KEEP YOUR
FINGER ON THE BOAT

This book belongs to

Linda

Cover Design and Portrait Sketch	Deborah Noble Finney Keosauqua, Iowa
Calligraphy	Mary J. Noble Douds, Iowa
Typography	Valeri K. Lantz Chicago, Illinois Sue Janes Kalamazoo, Michigan

Printed in the United States of America

-a𝖯

Order from	–ana Publishing Post Office Box 625 Kalamazoo, MI 49005

Debbie Noble

Keep Your Finger On the Boat

Lisa Pugh
and
Virginia Y. Pugh

-aP
–ana Publishing
Kalamazoo, Michigan

KEEP YOUR FINGER ON THE BOAT

Copyright 1990 by Virginia Y. Pugh

Library of Congress Catalog Card Number 89-84931
ISBN 0-942419-01-4
Printed in the United States of America

–ana Publishing
Post Office Box 625
Kalamazoo, Michigan 49005

FIRST EDITION

This book is dedicated to Linda, Ron, Dana and Mark, Lisa's brothers and sisters. They gave her more courage and more delight in living than they ever realized.

"Death is but crossing the world as friends do the seas; They live in one another still." William Penn (1644-1718)

With love and appreciation for those who walked this journey with Lisa and me: family, friends, our minister, our family physician, and especially Gene who was always there when we needed him; for the medical personnel at St. Jude Children's Research Hospital and Johns Hopkins Hospital; for Joseph V. Simone, M.D., Myrtle E. Felkner, Deborah Noble Finney and Mary J. Noble; and for Joyce, Myrt and Norma, without whose encouragement this book would not have been published.

Contents

Preface

Keep Your Finger On The Boat is a paradox. It is the very personal story of Lisa Pugh, a young girl who died of leukemia; but the story embodies much more that touches us deeply. Although it brings tears, her tragic death from her disease is the least universal aspect of her story. *Keep Your Finger On The Boat* evokes deeper and stronger emotions, and the easy recognition of familiar circumstances.

We watch an adolescent girl mature into a young woman with all the doubts, fears, love and courage amplified by her own strength in the face of suffering and death. We recognize her in our children and in ourselves. We give thanks that we haven't had to suffer her trial, and hope we would have met a similar challenge with her grace and dignity. As she observes in herself, and for us as well, the teenage conflict inherent in the child-adult causes anguish when she faces issues ranging from a "new outfit" to a serious illness—and everything in between.

Another consistent thread in the story's fabric is the importance of her family and social structure in providing the support she so obviously received. The dedication to her of her entire family exemplifies for us what we hope we would give and receive under comparably difficult circumstances. She drew sufficient strength from her family, friends and church to provide the emotional reserve that enabled her to write her diary, her poetry, her memories.

Whether or not these writings generate critical acclaim doesn't matter; the clarity of expression and the depth of feeling elevate the work to a stirring exclamation of courage. It is not an accident that this work can provide insight and inspiration to afflicted families and to those of us who work to ease their burdens. One senses that Lisa accepted the inevitability of her death long before she would admit it; that she was compelled by her love and compassion to speak to us and to open her heart, to take us inside. It is a rare and memorable experience to be so embraced.

Lisa writes three wishes near the end of her diary: "When I die, I want people to cry...because you'll miss a certain something I gave you each day." Wish fulfilled. "God, I hope I'm courageous...I want to die smiling, an inspiration to others." Also fulfilled. "If I could try three new things, they would be hang gliding, sky diving and flying (as a) pilot." Lisa, you soar with your story and carry us with you.

Joseph V. Simone, M. D., Director
St. Jude Children's Research Hospital
Memphis, Tennessee

Foreword

"Come, Courage, come and take me by the hand!
I have a long and weary way to go..." Clinton Scollard

That long and sometimes weary way began for Lisa Pugh one spring afternoon. It led her and her family from their home in Iowa to St. Jude Children's Research Hospital in Memphis, Tennessee, and finally to Johns Hopkins Hospital in Baltimore, Maryland.

Lisa's story is not a medical history; it is, rather, an account of the way one young woman summoned courage to live triumphantly and creatively, with the probable knowledge of an incurable disease. She shares with us her meetings with pain and her will to live positively. She was able to capsulize adolescence–with its accompanying uncertainties and identity crises–into a few years, while also developing a mature view of the meaning of her entire life and the possibility of approaching death.

This is, simply, Lisa's story as recorded in her diary, her tapes, her poetry and reminiscences, except for minor changes for purposes of clarity. Additions to it are excerpted from the journal and memories of her mother, Virginia.

Inevitably, questions must arise in the minds of those who knew, or now know through this book, the Pugh family: Could they possibly maintain any normalcy in their lives? Did the years of chemotherapy, during which a trip was made to St. Jude every month or six weeks, not drain them emotionally? And what of the long list of those whom they knew who had not won the battle, a list that grew ever longer, with attendant grief and uncertainty? How could a family sustain the events and stress over such lengthy periods?

What of the fear that Lisa's parents knew when she first returned to school, fear that she might be pushed, fall or otherwise be injured? In the summers following treatment, Lisa learned to water ski. Imagine the kind of parental self-control it must have taken to watch numerous tumbles into the water until finally, skittering and steadying and ultimately sailing, Lisa water skied! Lisa went camping, fished, drove the car and did many things that teenage girls do; and her family gave her total support in everything. We have to admire their steel-bright courage in allowing her to participate in life. Lisa had courage; certainly it was matched by, and perhaps born of, that of her family.

In her diaries, Lisa mentioned the "iron hand and lots of love" with which she and her siblings were raised. Yet, discipline never wavered because she was sick; she was not pampered.

Once Lisa expressed concern that so much of the family time and finances had to go to her, but her parents dealt with this easily: If one of the other four children had the same need, wouldn't she want the family's resources to go to the one needing them? This argument ended Lisa's guilt. This matter-of-fact and honest confrontation with every situation characterizes the Pugh family. Lisa was secure within its boundaries, secure enough to batter against it as she approached late teens.

Lisa had tremendous empathy for other people, far beyond her years; and she was willing to accept them as they were. She gained strength from others, often posted meaningful verses of poetry, scripture or inspirational writings on bulletin board or closet door, in her room at home or in the hospital.

The years of remission were also years of reflection for Lisa, filled with plans and dreams and yearnings, with feelings of excitement and nervousness over the St. Jude trips, all jumbling to keep emotions vacillating. For beneath everything was the truth that she had leukemia, and that no one had ever before remained in remission as long as she and her friends.

Two and a half years into remission, the first questionable cells were found in a bone marrow checkup at St. Jude. News of the finding was a terrible blow to the family, one of their darkest moments. The months that followed took all the courage that Lisa could muster, and were not without grief. Desperation and determination to meet the situation, whatever its course, walked hand in hand.

Lisa continued school during her junior year and shrugged, "It's nothing," with a typically quiet pride when she made Honor Society. But subsequent bone marrow tests confirmed the continued presence of questionable cells and evidence of a decline in the number of white blood cells needed to fight off infection. A sense of Lisa's uncertainty is reflected in her writings.

One of Lisa's greatest joys was writing, which often was punctuated with penciled faces for emphasis. She described her love of nature, her delight in animals, simple joys about small things, warm and dependent feelings for her family, even when, at times, despising that dependence. She addressed her journals to imaginary persons. We can only guess at her name choices, but we know of Lisa's word-awareness: Phoebe means shining; Felicia signifies happiness. Sometimes Lisa seemed caught up in her own story and the knowledge that she could never write its ending; but, with this book, she has become a published author.

Much of what Lisa left of herself to her family and friends is too intangible to be placed between the covers of a book, even though that book is hers. Lisa's words can teach us a lot about dying, and a lot about living. Perhaps this is her greatest gift to us all. And this she did leave to us, lovingly and freely: She shared the poignant journey that, in the end, we each must make alone.

Myrtle E. Felkner, Author
In the Wigwams of the Wyandott,
Making the Sunday School Better and
In the Beginning

A New Experience

"It takes both rain and sunshine to make a rainbow."

Author Unknown

It started when I was thirteen years old.* I can't say I'd like to do it again, but I believe that my family and I are closer and better for it.

On a Thursday in March, 19– I went to the doctor because I had a sore throat. I also had small, red spots and "growing" bruises on my legs. He said I had tonsillitis and should not go to school the next day. Then he sent me to the laboratory for blood tests.

Friday, the doctor called Mom and Dad into his office. He told them that I had leukemia and that the best place to go was St. Jude Children's Research Hospital in Memphis, Tennessee.

---

*This chapter includes Lisa's recounting of facts and feelings concerning her disease. From speeches made during remission to local school, church, service organizations and to a support group for St. Jude Children's Research Hospital, Lisa compiled her notes into a permanent record at age fifteen.

17

When they came home from the doctor's office, I was told. It's hard to say exactly what went through my mind when I heard the word "leukemia." I remember the moment and the words as if it had just happened five minutes ago, but I can't recall the thoughts that passed through my head. I didn't know much about it except it was often called "blood cancer" and was very serious. I think the word "cancer" really threw me. Friday night was spent in tears and a new closeness to my family. I feared that when I left the next morning I might never see my brothers and sisters again.

Saturday morning found us at the airport. Our minister and his wife were there to see us off. It was about four hours flying time to Memphis with a stop in St. Louis.

When we arrived at the hospital, we found a small and colorful building with a statue of St. Jude Thaddeus greeting us. We were in a strange city at a strange place, but this place was going to make me well again. It had to.

The people and personnel were so friendly and outgoing. In less than a half hour I was checked in, and into a room. There was the matter of medical history and blood tests and other routine procedures. We talked with the doctor and he told me I'd have a "bone marrow" and "lumbar puncture." Then, I didn't know what either phrase meant, so I placidly went along. Later, the mere mention of a "bone marrow" and "spinal tap" made me cry.

Supper came and finally it was time for Dad to go; Mom could stay the first night. I didn't sleep too well those first few nights, with all the lights and interruptions. More tests were run, resulting in the diagnosis of acute myelocytic leukemia; and the treatment I would follow was explained the next day.

St. Jude is not a remote institution in the South which serves only Southerners: there are doctors from all over the world—Brazil, Chile, the Philippines, India, Switzerland, Korea, Spain—as well as the United States. The resident who had checked me in that first day was a native of my home town! His mother and father were going to Cornell College at the time he was born, and his mother had grown up in Iowa. We discovered it was a small world, after all.

Monday was the first day I didn't feel well, and it took me six weeks to feel good again. Intravenous feedings through which the blood, platelets and medicines flowed were changed frequently. As I was in isolation, the nurses, doctors, Mom and Dad were the only contacts I had with the outside world. The "scenic view" from my window was a flashing Union Planters' Bank sign on top of a building and an Albert Pick Motor Inn rotating sign.

Happily, I *was* to see my brothers and sisters again. Ron, Dana and Mark came down with Dad one weekend, but Linda couldn't come because she was working. Though unable to be in my room, they stood on stools outside the window to visit with me. It was super to see them after three weeks, although there were two of everyone due to my double vision!

An abdominal infection complicated things. Due to extreme pain from that, I was given morphine. I had nightmares of spiders and of being locked in closets.

I want to go back:
Please! Let me go back.
I miss my brothers.
I miss my sisters.
I miss my father and my mother.
I miss the old ways,
Those were the good days.
Your new ways
Are bad ways
Oh-h-h! I want to go back.
PLEASE! Let me go back... Lisa

I used to get on a kick where I'd stick my tongue out at everyone–except Dr. A–, my doctor. I ordered the head nurse out of my room one day; I'll never forget. Later, she was my favorite nurse at St. Jude.

The thing that really kept me going was the mail and packages that people sent from home. I also remember long talks with Mom about everything and anything. She really became my closest *confidante.* I would dictate letters to her when I couldn't see or hold a pen, and she would write my friends for me. She was my eyes and right and left arms.

I remember very clearly going to the mirror to see myself when my hair started coming out because of my drugs. IT WAS A TRAUMATIC AND UNFORGETTABLE EXPERIENCE!!! ⊙⊙

Being in the hospital was not always dull and boring. Once in awhile there was plenty of excitement: I was eating soda crackers one night after Mom had gone, when the package fell on the floor. My IV had been taken out that day so I was able to crawl out and under the bed to retrieve the wrapper. When I was settled in bed again, the paper fell. I looked over the edge of the bed in time to see something skedaddle across the floor. I sat up and was very still for several minutes. Again I saw something come scurrying across the floor from the radiator. I looked under my bed and there sat a fat, brown mouse nibbling on the cracker crumbs.

I pulled the call cord and the desk nurse asked if she could help. I loudly announced that there was a mouse in my room, that I was scared, and to send someone–fast! I repeated this three times in about fifteen minutes before a nurse named Robbie came bustling into my room. I was nearly hysterical by now; and even if there had been a mouse in there before, I'd probably scared it into leaving.

> Stuck in a tree
> With a shake in his knee,
> The little mouse looked down at me.
> He glanced all around;
> Picked a leaf. With a bound
> He parachuted to the ground. Lisa

I was moved into another room for the night. I later found out the reason it took so long for someone to come: All the nurses except her were afraid to come, and she was busy in another room.

Robbie reminded me very much of a girl at home. We became great friends. On one return visit to St. Jude after being home, we were shocked to learn of her death. She had died of infectious hepatitis from a needle with which she had scratched her arm. After that, all needles were immediately disposed of in a special container.

After four treatments, one each week, I was in remission. The Friday night I found out, Mom and Dad were out eating. I had just eaten some Jello; and when Dr. A– broke the news to me, I became so excited I upchucked.

As soon as I was well enough to walk out by myself, I left Room 119 and went to the Medicenter, the residential facility for outpatients and their families, with Mom.

When I returned to the hospital for my first outpatient visit, we were told we could go home for awhile. Phase II was explained: My spleen would be removed; and I was introduced to my new doctor, Dr. J–. He carefully explained the surgical procedure and the treatment to follow.

Dad drove to Memphis to take Mom and me home. He had stayed the first two weeks and then had to go back.

I just couldn't get over the fact that I WAS HOME! When we first drove up in front of the house, there were signs across the front proclaiming "Welcome Home Ginny And Lisa" and "Welcome Home Lisa." I was really high! Friends came and went daily. The phone rang constantly.

In twelve days, I had another sore throat and we were on our way to Memphis again. They could determine nothing so we headed home. On the way, I started running a fever; but we kept on. We were there a couple of days when our doctor said that he thought we should head south again. My blood tests eventually showed positive for mono (infectious mononucleosis).

Well, I ended up in the hospital for about two weeks. My favorite diet consisted of baloney, tomato soup and grapefruit. My choices had the staff puzzled how I could manage these foods, since my throat was swollen nearly shut. I made a fairly speedy recovery and we went home again.

We hadn't been there any time at all when I started running a fever, and red spots appeared on my arms and torso. Once again we traveled south. They never did diagnose what I had, exactly, but I was a sight! They nicknamed me "salt and pepper," as the spots spread over my entire body and turned a purplish-blue color. I was nauseated, and it was discovered that my whole body chemistry was out of whack. Protein, vitamins and other vitals flowed day and night through an IV. However, when news came that Dad and Ron were coming down for the July 4th weekend, you can not possibly imagine how happy I was or how fast I felt better.

The day they were to arrive, I got my IV out. When they came, I sent them out to get pizza and ate so much that weekend, that afterward it didn't taste nearly so good.

This time I was in the hospital for three weeks; and when I got out, Mom and I stayed in Memphis for another week while I was an outpatient. Then, on a Sunday in mid-July, I was readmitted for the Phase II splenectomy scheduled for the next day.

Mom and Dad were both there. Surgery went well, although a fever of undetermined nature followed. I had not straightened one leg while in bed after surgery; so when I started to walk, it was with one bent leg. Two weeks later I walked out of the hospital minus 23 surgical clamps, wig case in hand. Somehow I had a feeling that I wouldn't be back there for a long time. At this time I was at my lowest weight, eighty pounds.

At home I was put on chemotherapy maintenance drugs: 6-MP pills every day and a weekly intravenous shot of ara-C. The pills were nothing bad so I didn't mind taking them. But that shot–that awful shot! It was something else.

It made me deathly ill, although part of it may have been psychosomatic. In fact, I used to get sick before I had the shot, sometimes. So, although my mind knew I wouldn't get sick every week–and my heart knew it–my stomach didn't seem to understand that message. I took my shot on Thursday nights; and because of the sedation I took with it, I missed Friday mornings at school. At least all this is a great way to get to know your doctor and all his office employees.

I remember some fellow patients at St. Jude: Cindy was a

year younger than I and had been diagnosed with acute myelocytic leukemia shortly before I was. We shared hospital stays as well as outpatient, clinic days for checkups. Our remissions and problems were similar, so we developed a real closeness with her and her family.

LouLou was a tiny, Black baby across the hall from my first room. His soft spot had never closed, and he was severely retarded. His mother had the same thing, and his father's whereabouts were unknown. His mother died while LouLou was at St. Jude, so he became an orphan. He was trainable, so several nurses worked constantly with him, trying to get him to smile, wave and walk in a baby walker, all of which he mastered. I never saw him again or learned what happened to him, but I'll never forget him.

David was a little three-year-old from Alabama. He had neuroblastoma, cancer of the nervous system. He was an extremely bright boy and brought much joy to those around him. Sometimes he was blind, losing all sight except for outlined shapes; at other times, vision was nearly normal. He didn't like people coming into his room because he thought they were there to hurt him. He suffered considerable pain from medicines and procedures used to help save his life. However, David passed on, leaving a world he had brightened with cheerfulness, to a new world. I hope he is keeping the angels and God happy, as he did so many people here.

Vincent was a teenage boy who had Hodgkin's disease. His mother was a chronic joker–really hysterical. One time she said that she and her husband had planned on four children, and the fourth one was triplets! True, too! Vincent graduated from high school and continued to do well.

Mrs. L– was a Mexican-American parent from New Mexico whose daughter had leukemia, too. I never met her Connie, but I heard a lot about her and became interested in her case. Mrs. L– was another jester, always giggling. She had this thing about racing me down the hall, though clearly I was in no shape for athletics. I came to love her; and even after the death of Connie when we lost face-to-face contact, I still wrote to her regularly, and she was omnipresent in my thoughts and prayers.

Jenny of Arkansas and her Mom were among my favorite people, too. Her mother was a widow and had brought Jenny to St. Jude with some serious thyroid problems. Jenny was the same age as my brother Mark, which may have been one reason for our early attachment. In the years afterward, we often left gifts and letters for each other at the hospital, on our checkup trips.

Another first friend at St. Jude was Paula, also from Arkansas. She had lymphocytic leukemia and was taking radiation when we first knew her. She was always so peppy and smiling, even when she didn't feel too well. Paula and I were the same age, and we sort of hit it off right from our first meeting.

Juliann was a college friend of my mother, very handicapped as a result of polio in her late twenties. She lived in Memphis, and we usually had dinner together when there. It was really neat to see how cheerful and hospitable she and her husband were, and I felt I could do as well as she. I resolved to keep a smile on and not to give in.

There were so many others that helped me through those first weeks, but these were a few of the special ones.

I started school that year along with everyone else. My previous school work and grades convinced my counselor and teachers that I could go on to the eighth grade, even though I had missed a whole quarter of seventh grade. I hardly slept on the eve of the first day of school. My heart raced and my stomach was full of butterflies from the anticipation of seeing all my friends again. I don't think I had ever said "Hi" to so many people in one day in my whole life. I was surprised I wasn't hoarse the next day. My having lost 45 pounds was a source of several comments.

There were three stages I went through in getting back into the social swing: The first was one of being eyed, curiously. The air was filled with unasked questions and a feeling of being thought of as "ill." I always felt like people were thinking, *So this is what a person with leukemia looks like.* I tried to ignore it, but it's not something you can forget about without working at it.

Next was a period of feeling people were liking me, or

being friends with me, out of pity. In talking to a couple of friends, I found this to be anything but true; but it took more than hearing this to make me believe it.

Finally was the feeling of being one of the gang again. My friends didn't treat me differently. They asked questions that had gone unanswered for so long, and understood if I wasn't able to do all the things they did. I think this phase and the final acceptance of my disease went hand in hand. They were close in happening, chronologically speaking.

In October I was a bridesmaid, along with my sister Dana, in our sister Linda and Bob's wedding. The dress I wore had to be altered considerably from the pattern. I had my wig cleaned for the occasion, and I sat on a decorated stool for the ceremony.

In November I finally went to school without a wig. Except for those who knew I'd been wearing one, people simply thought I had my hair cut.

I missed school the month of December due to a "spinal" headache, a problem which sometimes followed the spinal taps to check for leukemia cells. It was gone in time for Christmas, thank goodness.

During our St. Jude visit in February, Dr. J– broke the news to Mom, Dad and me that he would be leaving there in March to head up the Sickle Cell Anemia research in Washington, D. C. He had become very interested in the study of this disease while at St. Jude. We were all very sad to hear he was leaving, but he assured us that he would return if the red tape became too much–and that he would certainly keep tabs on me. After Dr. J– went to D. C., we corresponded occasionally.

People sometimes asked me what I thought about having a Black doctor. I never really gave it any thought; I loved Dr. J–. He was part of my "family"–and he made several outstanding contributions to St. Jude medical science. I would have loved to have seen him anytime, and just to talk.

Well, Dr. J–'s departure meant I'd be having *another* doctor. When I was introduced to Dr. Simone, I was apprehensive; but later I could truthfully say I admired him just as much as my two previous doctors.

In April I developed infectious hepatitis and spent ten days, with Mom, in Memphis as an outpatient. That passed quickly, although I was somewhat physically exhausted. I finished the eighth grade going half-days.

As summer rolls around and school is closed for the year, families pack for their long-awaited vacations. Our family has been camping ever since I was eight months old. We've roughed it in the woods for two or three weeks every summer–no telephones, no TV, no fancy clothes, no running water.

Usually we didn't get started on time because something in the preliminaries went awry. One summer Dad backed the van, to which the boat was cartopped, into the garage. It seemed the garage was lower than he estimated.

Another time we were only forty-five miles out of town, heading for Glacier Park, when smoke came pouring in through the back window from the trunk. Dad had dropped a pipe ash while checking the shock absorbers. We lost several pieces of camping gear, a lot of food and a day of vacation because we had to return home for the night.

All tires expire at some time; but we can drive a whole year without a flat, only to have one on vacation. Once we were near the top of one of the Big Horn Mountains in Wyoming when a trailer tire blew out. On a gravelly, hairpin road in above one hundred degree heat, with me carsick in the back seat, my Dad and brothers changed the tire while we all prayed another car wouldn't come by.

Once we started a middle-of-the-night trek across the Nevada desert, seven of us packed like sardines into the Ford. There had been the usual quarrel over who was going to sit where and who would get which window. Finally we were settled, but five of us kids intended to stay awake through the night. Soon, however, a chorus of snores and a blissful calm fell upon our parents' ears as the squabbling and squirming halted.

Later, Dad decided to stop and rest; but as soon as the motor was off, six pairs of eyes popped open–along with half a dozen mouths.

Dawn was approaching. When the first hint of light appeared behind the curtain of mountains, instantaneous quiet fell over the car; and fourteen eyes were glued on the horizon. Slowly the ball of fire rose. The sky flamed orange, amber and violet; and the black mountains became emerald as they were illuminated by the early morning light. Darkness unwrapped to reveal a sand-studded desert. Dawn broke.

We had a major disaster when all our camping equipment was stolen. We had returned late at night from a trip and left everything in the garage, except for food and clothes packed in the boat. Next morning, only the boat remained. Two tents, a tarp, stove, lantern, six sleeping bags, life jackets, the motor and everything else—missing.

Vacation is putting up with your brothers and sisters for a couple of weeks. This includes taking your sister fishing. This may not sound too awful, but it is when I want to enjoy myself. I have to bait her hook because she won't touch the worm. I have to take the fish off, too, because God forbid that she should touch such an indelicate creature.

One day we were out on the lake and she caught a twenty-inch sucker, an inedible fish that cleans the bottom of the lake. She was yelling, "It's a big one!" when she hooked it; but when she saw the ugly thing coming up over the side of the boat, she screamed bloody murder, stood up and flung it at me, hitting me in the face. I almost kept the fish and threw her overboard. ;-

With no movies or TV, nightly entertainment becomes a test of one's imagination. One must be shrewd and eavesdrop on other campers to find out what they did last night: "We went to the dump and watched the bears." So once, we too decided to have a night on the town dump. We waited until it was dark, parked on the dump road and waited for the bears. The only thing that showed in two hours was a horde of bats.

Sitting in a tight circle around one campfire, we gazed without blinking into the yellow-orange fingers of flame. Our eyes caught the reflection of the blossom of fire and sparkled in its brilliance. Quietly, on padded paws, an inky-black creature with a virginal-white racing stripe down its back moseyed out of the velvety darkness into the fireside ring. We all sucked in our breath quickly and became instant statues until the evening's unscheduled star made its final exit.

It's a shame everybody doesn't have the opportunity to spend a week roughing it.

In July I had another "spinal" headache, while we were on vacation NO LESS! The headache was not as persistent as the one in December and lasted about a week. I would lie in the fishing boat during the day. At night I brought a cushion from the trailer out and lay by the fire.

The park was wrapped in the velvety blackness of night. Crickets and bullfrogs began their chirping and croaking serenade. The air smelled of smoky bonfires that dotted the darkness. The aroma of fish entrails burned the nostrils. Children were tucked into toasty warm sleeping bags while grown-ups chatted softly around the campfire. A few campers bustled one last time up the path, flashlights swinging at their sides. The crescent moon's reflection lay weakly on the lake, while its distant relatives twinkled in the twilight. A cool, refreshing breeze whistled through the trees, and campers scurried to dowse their fires. Then, all was calm.

A furry, masked bandit of night
Cleverly robs the garbage cans.
What happens when you shine a light on him?
He stares at you,
His expression indignantly saying,
"How dare you disturb me?"
He's a clean fellow,
Always washing his food before supping.
His looting is usually a family affair;
Wife and children accompany him.
Quiet he is not.
Someday he'll get caught. Lisa

Healthwise, everything went exceptionally well after July. The following school year, I missed classes only for our trips to Memphis every six weeks. I accompanied fellow ninth-graders to Chicago on a fun field trip in May; and had been track manager for the girls' team, which took the city championship, in the spring. On the last day of ninth grade, and junior high, I was proud to receive an athletic letter with "Mgr" printed on it. I also received a scholastic award of outstanding merit.

In August, though, I came down with pneumocystis pneumonia and spent three and a half weeks in the hospital. High temperatures and chills made this stay an unpleasant one. It made me ill to think about the fact that my hair had-n't been washed for a long time—and that I was losing my fantastic tan! The oxygen mask was uncomfortable, and I couldn't read because I couldn't wear my glasses. I wore the mask for three weeks, and couldn't even get out of bed for two and a half. Once, I was mistakenly released from isola-tion, so I went out and phoned Dad and walked up and down the halls.

On our flight home, the stewardesses and agents were really helpful: I was carried on and off the plane and had a wheel chair at each terminal. Dana, Mark, Dad and Grandma were at the airport to greet us. It felt good to be home again, even though I had missed the opening of school. A cake was waiting; and the next day, several friends came to see us.

After two weeks, we went back to Memphis for my check up. The doctors said I had recovered much better than expected. My lungs were completely clear, and I was to get a full dose of ara-C. We stayed an extra night due to the shot. On the way home I didn't feel too well, and the next day I developed jaundice. Our local physician called Dr. Simone, but we didn't have to go back to St. Jude—our doctor took care of me at home. I got terribly yellow, though; and, natu-rally, a fever accompanied it.

Since we had returned from that check up, I had been on a teach-a-phone. It helped a lot in keeping up with school work. Even after I was over the hepatitis, I had to wait to go back to school since so much mono, colds and flu were going around; however, in November I finally started half days.

> For my birthday I got a rose
> And it was a beautiful, red, American Beauty rose.
> I put it in a rosebud vase
> And set it in my window.
> I admired
> And never tired
> Of admiring it.
> Then a friend came.
> She was sad and unsmiling.
> I showed her my rose
> And she said
> It was a beautiful, red, American Beauty rose.
> I took the rose from its vase
> And gently placed it in my friend's hands.
> Her sad, unsmiling face
> Smiled and looked happy.
> She admired
> And never tired
> Of admiring it. Lisa

Mom, Dad and I went to Memphis in November, too, and were told that on our next visit, if everything checked out OK, I would be taken off the medications. Dr. Simone said that the hepatitis probably had been caused from the ara-C therapy and that my liver function studies had not yet returned to normal. He also said that I had been in remission for over two and a half years, and that the risks of continuing treatment balanced those of discontinuing it.

There were four of us who would be trying this procedure of stopping treatment. This was a "first" for St. Jude Hospital because no other group of kids had responded so well to any kind of treatment for myelocytic leukemia.

You can imagine how I felt! No, I don't think anyone who hasn't been through it all can even feel a hint of what I felt that day. Those next three weeks of waiting were the slowest ever!

Well, things did check out; and by late November, I, along with Cindy, Glenda and Ginger, were off all drugs. We all felt the same relief and excitement–NO MORE SHOTS! Unbelievable! I was on Cloud 9 that day, and so were our parents and families.

There were three stages I went through to get to the point where I fully accepted my having leukemia. The first phase was disbelief: This can't be happening to me. It's just a bad dream and I'll wake up in a moment. I couldn't, or wouldn't, believe that this terrible disease was in me.

In the second stage I cursed the "people" who gave me this disease. I was full of hatred for it and viewed it as an unfair burden placed on my shoulders by some terrible persons.

The final step was acceptance: I have the disease and I'll always have it, so I might as well make the best of the situation. I was able to talk about it without any inhibitions.

As I look back over everything, I just sit and marvel at what has happened these past two years and eight months: We have met some of the most laudable doctors and nurses anywhere and have come to know so many new, charming, positively beautiful friends. We have learned that no matter if luck and everything else seems against you, your friends and family are always there to make the rough riding smoother and to make the worst not so bad, after all.

I've learned that there is a little bit of good in everything, no matter how bad it may seem. Like, we would never have known what a beautiful place St. Jude is; neither would a lot of people whom we've told, and we wouldn't have had a tour of Tennessee. I might be a pudgy 125 pounds, or more; and my hair still would be mousey brown and very straight.

If there was ever any doubt in my mind before, there certainly isn't now–that there is a God and He is taking care of all His children, and He does hear our prayers.

I've learned that there are so many good people we never hear or know about, and that the world isn't all bad: There still is a lot of love.

Most of all, I've learned that faith, hope and a smile is what it takes to keep your chin up and know that everything is going to be just fine, even when it may be your darkest hour.

St. Jude is a place where the impossible happens. I thank God for it, and I thank Danny Thomas for making possible a hospital like it. His love and ambition have built an institution of world-renown.

I have so much to be thankful for as I start a new chapter in my book of life.

Happiness is...
walking in the woods, talking to a friend, breathing the
    mountain air,
seeing a puppy born, smiling,
feeling a fuzzy duckling, tasting some cool lemonade,
hearing from far-away friends, smelling a rose,
    caring for a sick child,
accepting the bad with the good, helping someone,
learning something new every day, sharing a secret,
remembering a birthday, forgetting spilt milk, doing
    small favors,
giving a kiss, holding a hand.
Happiness is loving. Happiness is living. Lisa

To Mom and Dad with love...
With whom I've shared many smiles
and many tears.

Dear Phoebe

"We can complain because the rose bush has thorns, or we can rejoice because the thorn bush has roses."

Author Unknown

December 31, 19– Tonight I feel excited for the incoming year. I hope the rest of the year I'll be able to be in school. I'm not ready for vacation to end: I hope to spend some time in Iowa City with Ron. I hope Linda and Bob have a baby. Mark is really growing up, more bearable every day. And Dana grows more like Mom every day. Dear God, make this a blessed New Year, in every sense of the word. I love everyone so much.

I'm sixteen. Three years ago I found out I had leukemia. When I had to go to a hospital almost six hundred miles from home, Dad usually had to return; but Mom stayed with me.

The following two chapters contain Lisa's journals, written or tape-recorded, which were begun soon after her sixteenth birthday and were addressed to fictitious confidants, Phoebe and Felicia.

She had to leave my two brothers and two sisters, one of whom was getting married. Although Mother wasn't there, she still helped to plan the wedding. She also left behind her job as teacher and director of a preschool.

The night we found out I was sick–even though she was really upset and had a lot on her mind–Mom called neighbors, relatives, friends and the minister, made arrangements for her school, and tried to reassure me and the rest of the family. Even then she was thinking of others.

Several times when I became seriously ill, Mom stayed round the clock, often sitting up in a chair to sleep. She kept the family posted with phone calls and letters. Once when I had a bad virus, Mom was at the hospital by herself; and I never knew until later how scared she was, because she is so strong.

When I came home for the first time, Mom gave up some of her favorite activities to be constantly by my side. She wouldn't even leave long enough to go to the grocery store.

When I started back to school, she let me know where I could get hold of her, in case I got too tired. Later, she told me how worried she was if I should fall while going up and down stairs; but at the time, she never let on.

Mom tried to let me do what I wanted, although she wouldn't let me do everything. I used to get mad, but now I see she did everything in my best interests.

It's hard for some to imagine not being able to walk, or to go up a curb. Mom never got impatient when I couldn't do these things and never minded that sometimes she had to help me. She was my hands when I couldn't use them, my legs when I couldn't walk and my eyes when I couldn't see.

Sometimes I'd be depressed. Mom was always there to whisper just the right words of encouragement. I was positive because she was positive. I couldn't have made it without her and her continued love, hope, faith and courage.

Mom is forever by me. She's the girl in my life.

January 10. They say that when you write a diary, you lack something. Can't remember what it is you lack. I keep a diary because I don't have a friend to whom I can say all things. I have friends to whom I talk seriously, but not one that I can tell *all* my secrets.

January 12. Dear Phoebe, I feel like crying. We stopped to get the film of Christmas and my birthday party and, most disappointing, the four of us girls in remission–and of Dr. Simone. They ruined the film while processing. We won't ever be together anymore, either.

January 19. I wrote a dumb letter to Ron: I asked him what he would do and how he would feel if I relapsed. He never did answer it, but we talked later.

April 3. I'm just furious. When I think or learn of more and more people getting involved in the drug scene, I just want to scream. I wish sometimes that everyone who is a drug freak would have to depend on drugs for their lives, for one week. Then maybe they'd realize what a mistake they're making. I wish they knew what it is like to know that the only reason you're alive is because you took pills every day for two and a half years, and a shot once a week for that long, especially when it makes you so sick. I hated that shot.

April 10. Today was my teacher Evelyn's funeral, and the minister gave an excellent service. I remember how she helped me explain my leukemia and the treatment to my phys. ed. class when I first went back to school. How ironic that now she has died from cancer. She had a husband and five boys–everything to live for.

And there's Kim, my classmate who died with a tumor. Kim hadn't even begun her life. Over and over, I keep remembering her sister's words to me, "You're the lucky one of the three."

All three of us fighting cancer, and I'm the only one who's still here. I'm doing so well; I keep thinking, *Why me?* It's a pity all three of us won't be together on earth again; but we'll be together in eternity, and that's the important point. That's all I'm thinking about.

April 13. Well, I've been to Memphis and back. I had a good report, but it was a sad trip in another way: We were told that Cindy had relapsed. Did my heart race to hear that!

It really made me stop and think. We knew this might happen, but I never thought it would. I'm a little scared.

> ...I will not doubt, though sorrows fall like rain,
> And troubles swarm like bees about a hive;
> I shall believe the heights for which I strive,
> Are only reached by anguish and by pain;
> And, though I groan and tremble with my crosses,
> I yet shall see, through my severest losses,
> The greater gain.... Ella Wheeler Wilcox

June 11. Dear Phoebe, I've been fairly busy all day and kind of secluded, but now I'm a "melancholy baby." I broke my fingernail and didn't get any sympathy! I'm sorry; I haven't been like this. It's probably because I'm tired. My resolution to keep smiling is only 50-50.

I feel weird tonight: I wish I could go away by myself and nobody'd bother me. I'm going to bed now so I can get up and get in a full day tomorrow.

I can't wait for Michelle to come. We used to have so much fun together. Always had time for good, long talks and making school plans. Why did she have to move to St. Louis? I'm missing her more than I ever thought I would.

June 23. My best friend Sue has a boyfriend. I find myself a little envious. That's one of the things I wish for most. I often wonder if I'll ever have one, because of my leukemia. Maybe not. I wish no one knew I had it. But it's part of me and people have to accept it along with me. I tell myself "Someday..." but a little voice in the back of my consciousness says, "No." It's a fact I'll have to face.

I miss Dana more than I can ever put into words, and she's only been gone to school a week. I try to do things for Mom that she did, but I have to force myself because I don't enjoy doing them. I cry sometimes, even though I try so hard not to. I love her.

I have been so tired; I can't figure it out. I get nine to eleven hours of sleep almost every night, but I'm exhausted by the end of the day—and sometimes by noon.

I'm so excited. I'm going to have a surprise anniversary party for Mom and Dad. Ron and his girlfriend are taking them out to eat; and when they come home, some of their friends will be here for dessert. I hope it works out. I'll either have to make the dessert and hide it, or keep it in someone else's refrigerator. Won't it be neat, Phoebe?

I'm so mixed up. I love being a teenager, but it's so confusing. I want my youth, but I also want my adulthood. My mind and feelings are so contorted at times: I feel like I'm on a merry-go-round.

Time marches by;
The months and years they fly.

The seasons come and go;
In the wind they blow.

Time stands still in
Idle hours and anticipation,
Yet slides by in titillation.

A parent's time is short until
Their youngsters' childhood years abort.
Then, before it's even known,
It seems they all have grown,
Left home to make it on their own.

A child's carefree years
Are few before he has
Responsibilities to pursue.

Time runs out for some;
For others, it's just begun.

Time turns in a circle, unbroken,
Leaving the past as a token
Of time gone by. Lisa

July 5. I have such terrible news: and I really don't want to write, but I want to know my reactions later. We were in Memphis the past two days. Although the trip fared well for me, it didn't for two of the people we've known and come to love down there. We hadn't seen Holly since last fall, but Dr. Simone said she was doing OK about three months ago. When we asked about her, we found out she had died. I still haven't grasped that.

Then, the most terrible: Cindy! Cindy, who was in the hospital most of the time I was; who was so cheerful; who demanded her way–and usually got it. Cindy, whom we stopped to see last summer on vacation; who suffered her shots and disliked them as much or more than I did; who had hepatitis like me; who went off medications with me. Cindy who, when relapsed, believed remission could happen again. *That* Cindy lay dying this time; and I think it's rotten, terrible, horrible news.

I've cried until I don't think there's another tear, but my heart is bleeding still. They couldn't get her to respond to any of the drugs, so now they've stopped everything and are just keeping her comfortable. No IV's or anything. And I can't believe it. I'm fighting off tears thinking about it. Why Cindy? It's so unfair! Her whole family was there, and Mom said she'd probably live another day or so. Why does anyone have to die at age fifteen?

July 8. I'm in the weirdest mood I can ever remember. I took the car and just drove, not knowing where I was going. I had a long talk with Ron, and I really feel a bunch better now. I have asked myself, "Who am I?" and have said that I hated me.

I don't really hate myself. I just want to be so perfect; and I can't be, any more than anyone else. Sometimes I think I'm either just a name and face with empty insides or Lisa Pugh, the girl with leukemia. I am not sick! I wish I could be a normal person. It doesn't bother me one iota that I have it because I understand it, or think I do. And others, even Mom and Dad, don't. If they understood, I'd feel so much better.

I guess this is the identity crisis I've read so much about. Right now I don't know where I am or where I'm going. I *refuse* to live in the past. From now on, there is no "before I was sick" or "after I got sick." Today is the day. I have so much energy. Think positive. I can do it. I will do it! I've used having this disease as an excuse for too long. So, I can't take phys. ed. So can't a lot of others who don't have leukemia. Enuf!

July 27. I'm on vacation at Razorback Lake, Phoebe. Vacation is for relaxation; my favorite way to relax is fishing. Like all enthusiasts, I sit in the boat dreaming of the big one I'm going to catch, while day after day I don't even get a nibble.

This lazy afternoon I lay broiling in our fourteen-foot Alumi-Craft with two things etched in my mind: a suntan and a fish feast. I could see the steam rising from the lake. I was glad I'd shoved the bait under the seat to prevent having fried worms. The water was serene, except for several million waterbugs skating over the surface. I sprawled on the back seat, face up, my feet dangling over the starboard side. In my hand I grasped my trusty Zebco equipped with a hook, line, sinker and bobber for early detection of a nibble. In my ears was the monotonous drone of pesky mosquitoes.

Then it came. At first it was a small twitch; and I lay motionless, poised for more. Then there was a tug. I jerked the pole upwards to insure snagging my prey. I clenched the rod in my right hand while I placed the landing net within reach. I slowly reeled in my whopper, letting it play at the end of the line. As it surfaced, I armed myself with the huge net. I lifted my line out of the water and swung it into the net. My gigantic fish slipped through the one-inch hole of the netting. It was a whole three inches long and had swallowed the hook, no less!

Back on shore, I was hounded by, "How many did you catch?"

"None, but you should have seen the monster that got away!"

Once, after a week without a fish dinner, a fellow camper went out in waders about a hundred yards from shore and caught a like-record muskie. It's hard to be friendly with people like that!

I'm sure glad Dana could come with us to the lake. Seeing her again is just great. I remember when she and I befriended a neighboring camper one time when we were in Minnesota. The three of us were practicing acrobatics. I started to do a handspring over our new friend's back, but failed and landed on my hand. Looking down, I saw the middle finger on my right hand jutting backwards from the second joint.

I ran to Mom shouting, "My finger is broken," but she continued to read until I shoved my L-shaped finger under her nose. *Then* she leaped to action, dragging me to surrounding campsites, exclaiming that I had broken my finger.

A camper volunteered to drive us to the hospital thirty miles away because Dad and the boys had taken our car to another lake to fish. I wailed the entire trip. The doctor diagnosed the finger as "just dislocated" and snapped it back in place.

I sure have missed Dana. I really hate to go home and miss her again.

July 29. We returned home from vacation today and had bad news waiting for us: Cindy's family had written that she died the day after we were in Memphis. Now the waiting and not knowing is over, although it's still a great shock. I knew and was expecting she would die; but my subconscious kept saying "Maybe something...." So, I really hadn't fully accepted it. She has been in my thoughts and prayers so much. Now she's at home forever.

Think of stepping on shore
And finding it Heaven.
Of taking hold of a hand
And finding it God's hand.
Of breathing a new air
And finding it celestial air.
Of feeling invigorated
And finding it immortality.
Of passing from storm and tempest
To perfect calm.
Of waking and knowing
I am home. Author Unknown

July 30. I really feel good, although I *should* feel guilty. I had the car and went to the library, the mall and downtown. I wasn't supposed to go there, but I went down to see Sue. I lied to Mom; that's why I feel guilty. I *never* lie to her. Maybe once won't matter; and besides, I'll probably confess. And...I found this outfit I want badly!

People fascinate me, Phoebe. Many of my idle moments are spent watching anyone in sight and speculating about their personalities. I have several different games I play. The most fun is trying to decide if people look like their names; or if I don't know them, trying to guess what name they look like.

Two of the best places to go people-watching are the zoo and restaurants. The zoo is more interesting, the folks more than the animals; and I'd rather gaze at people walking freely than at animals pacing behind bars. It's an ideal place to categorize and compare persons: How many pregnant women? barefoot kids? fat people? Or which animals do I think people would most enjoy seeing? People even look a lot like dogs and other domestics, as well as wild animals. Sometimes they resemble their pets.

In a restaurant, I can tell about someone by what she/he orders, how she handles the waitperson, his table manners and, if I'm close enough, by conversations.

I like to see people as characters from novels I've read, search for physical features like "a dark beauty" or "smiling eyes."

I know a lot of people I don't know. 😊

August 11. We had such a great weekend, camping with friends at Rathbun Lake. Spent most of it playing cards because it rained. Bill and I traded insults the whole time. It's funny. He and I have been friends since forever, it seems. Well, since childhood anyway. We've always had such great times, but now it's different. Like we're suddenly new friends. He treats me like Lisa, not like a girl with leukemia–as so many do. He's a pretty special guy. I wish he didn't live so far away.

6'3"
173 lbs.
Born July 3
Horoscope sign: Cancer
Blood type: A+
My dream. 😊

> A dream is something you can have
> To keep within your heart;
> To build on when you're sad
> Or your whole world's been torn apart.
> May all your dreams
> Bloom like daisies in the sun;
> May you always have stars in your eyes;
> May you not stop running
> Until your race is won;
> And may you always have blue skies.
>
> Camp Fire Song, Author Unknown

August 14. I'm packing for our Memphis trip. Really dreading it this time; I don't want to be reminded of Cindy.

August 17. Some good news and some bad. A lot has happened since Thursday night. First the bad: I had a bone marrow and spinal tap. Then I had another bone marrow because the first didn't have enough cells. Then I had pulmonary function and arterial blood gas tests. Ginger relapsed about two weeks ago.

We left St. Jude about 4:00 p. m. with my arm unusable and two aching hips. Called Michelle when we got to St. Louis. No answer. Her not being home was the straw that broke the camel's back. I cried and felt emotionally drained.

The worst news: I might be going to relapse. I had two or three cells in my marrow. It might be nothing. Probably is, since my blood counts are *par excellent* and I feel super.

The good news: Glenda is still doing excellently.

Oh, I'm so scared, Phoebe. We have to go back in two weeks. I wish the time was up so we'd know for sure. But I'm not going to think about it. I've gone through a lot more than this and never relapsed; and this has happened before and nothing came of it. Nothing else shows any indication of being wrong.

Even if it is, they'll whip it. I know they can.

I wish I could have talked to Dr. Simone, but he was in the hospital for his own surgery. He always makes me feel better. I felt better after talking to Sue when we got home. I'm praying, believe me.

"I prayed to the Lord, and He answered me;
He freed me from all my fears." Psalm 34:4.

August 18. I babysat tonight for Evelyn's brother-in-law's family. They told me how much my letters meant to her. She kept them in her Bible. That makes me feel so good to know I helped her; she did so much for me at school. Hard to realize that she has been dead four months already. I'm glad I knew her.

August 25. We took Dana to college and had a tearful goodbye. Really going to miss her. School starts tomorrow for me, my junior year.

August 28. Just a quickie before I pack. We go to Memphis tomorrow, and I'm confident nothing will be wrong. I keep telling myself that, anyway. I'm just minutely scared, but my second mind says everything will be fine.

August 29. As the day grows nearer, I have more apprehension than I thought. My second mind still says everything will be perfect, but I'm nervous anyhow and will feel better when I know for sure.

I'll tell you one thing, Phoebe: Under no circumstances am I staying. No way! I've got too much school to go to. I'm going home with or without their consent, one way or the other. *Pray.*

August 30. Everything was FINE! Dad about fainted, and we all were smiles. I knew all along everything would be okay. 🙂

September 12. I'm in the awfullest mood: I've grumped at everyone today. I don't know why, other than I'm fatigued. I hope it's better tomorrow.

October 17. Well, Phoebe, all these days for almost a year now I've been writing to you, but I've always thought as if I've been talking to you. I always wanted to talk to you and now I can, with this tape. I don't know who you are, but I know who I want you to be.

I saw a movie tonight called "Sunshine," and it was about a girl named Kate. She had a rare kind of cancer and she was dying. She was in love and she had a little girl; and she was leaving tapes for her baby. She married the guy that she loved; they had a beautiful relationship. The movie was super-sad, just terrible.

It sort of hit home. I guess you could say that I realize that some day I'm going to be Kate, lying in that bed, dying. In the movie they said dying is harder for those who watch than the act of dying actually is. I don't know; I think that's true. So I decided I wanted to leave something in this world more tangible than pieces of paper with writing on them, and the movie told me a way I could do that: Leave a tape with my voice on it. I'm going to make one, or several, and keep them for when I'm gone.

It's hard to have leukemia—or any disease. Hard because you're different. No matter how much you're the same, you're different. People don't accept that. They look at you funny, or bombard you with questions. I really don't mind all that; it's just that sometimes I feel as if people like me out of pity, and I won't have that. I'll have their genuine friendship, but I won't have their pity.

Don't walk in front of me–I may not follow.
Don't walk behind me–I may not lead.
Walk beside me and just be my friend. Albert Camus

I have a name and a face, and I have feelings. Feelings are hard to live with sometimes.

Me!
I am unique:
No one looks like me;
No one thinks like me.
I am my own person;
I am what I choose to be.
I have my very own fingerprint.
Like a snowflake
I have no twin.
I don't claim to be perfect,
But I'm the best I can be.
Every star has its place
Mine is here. Lisa

At times I wish it were over, but other times I wouldn't give up living for anything.

I have a beautiful family and beautiful friends; and it's hard to think of going on, into another world, without them. But I live with that fact every day, in the back of my mind. It's not something you can push out or ignore. It's always there: Some day I'm going to die.

To quote a book I read once: "If I don't die of it, I'll surely die with it." I'd rather die of it, I think, than to think I've come this far–to be killed accidentally, or just to die of natural causes. I'd rather die *of it.*

I have decided: I have so much to offer from the study of my body after I'm gone, for what they can find out about leukemia. I see no point in putting my body into the ground in a useless casket that costs a lot of money. I want my body to go to science. They can learn more from me than the ground can.

I do a lot of thinking that's hard to write because I don't

write the way I talk. These tapes are going to be a lot of help. There's so much to say; there's no where to start. I guess I'd better go to bed for now, but I'll talk to you either tomorrow or some day soon. And thanks for listening, Phoebe.

October 19. Tonight I'm going to talk about the future, something that I dwell on quite a bit. A lot of people don't even consider their future; and, you know, I find that hard to grasp. I can't believe that they go through their lives just taking it day by day. I think you have to think about the future; you have to know what you're going to do. You can't just go into it cold.

Part of the reason I have always planned my future is that I have such a sharp, "visible" picture of what I want it to be. Sometimes I think that even if I don't get there, I've had it. Really, I feel I have. I've imagined it, but I've known it. So, if it doesn't turn out the way I planned, or if I don't have a future, well, I *have* had one—in my mind.

I live in my mind, too. I have to have things in mind before I can live them. So, in a sense, I live day-to-day, too. For instance, I'm pretty sure I want to go to Simpson College. I'd like to see the campus first; but that's where I want to go to major in French and language arts, and to get a teaching certificate.

I want to spend my junior year abroad, either in Brittany or the Basque country. I'd like to see Paris, but I wouldn't want to stay there. And when I'm through with college, I'd like to teach English to the French or translate books, or something else along the language arts line.

Well, I'm really tired. I went horseback riding yesterday so I'm very sore! I went to the store today and bought Ben Gay, so I think I'll quit for tonight. But I had been thinking about my future and thought I'd just put it down as something to save. G'night.

October 23. (Sigh) Well, Phoebe, I've jotted down a few things I want to tell you. I haven't been taping for a few days, but I have things on my mind.

Probably the one that I should talk about first, because it bothers me the most, is that Homecoming is Saturday and I'm not going—which doesn't really surprise me. I don't know what's wrong, but it upsets me. It's not that I want to go to Homecoming as much as the fact that everybody else is going, and I feel left out.

Everybody is talking about the dress they're wearing and the flowers they're going to get, where they got their shoes, and who they're going with, or if they really want to go with this person. All that stuff. It's upsetting to be the odd man out: I guess you could say that. I hate being outside of the action. Soooo...I'm upset about it. Sue knows, but she tries not to talk about it. And she doesn't, which helps.

Oh, guess what! *This* is so exciting! Friday, I'm going to see "Gone With The Wind." It starts today and I cannot wait. Oh, Rhett Butler. Oh, Scarlett, eat your heart out. I just loved Rhett in the book. Scarlett–Oh, she made me so mad. I just can't wait to see Clark Gable (pant, pant) Rhett Butler–I can't wait!

Alrighty. Next note is my big ambition: To write the great American novel. I want to do that so badly, but it takes so much to write a book–study and all. And authors all have such terrible lives. I guess I've had too good a life: I'm not old enough to have experienced all there is in life. It takes more experiences than mine to be able to write a book; but oh, golly, I do want to write one. A romantic novel.

I've been thinking, Phoebe, that you're kind of like my friend when I was little. I used to have this pretend playmate. Her name was Barbara and she was like my conscience. Because anything I did wrong, Barbara would say, "Lisa, Lisa." I used to talk to her; we were best buddies, you know? Best buddies. For someone who isn't there, I mean, that's pretty good. Well, tonight I remembered a girlfriend named Barbara, who wasn't even a girl: She was just an imaginary person. G'night.

November 5. (Singing) Dear, dear Phoebe. Tonight I'm going to talk about Sue. I wish I could tell you just how much she means to me. It's hard to tell anybody. I've never felt this way toward anyone before.

I tell her often what a good friend she is. I hope she believes that; I think she does. You hear people say words

48

like that all the time, but you don't know what they're thinking. Sue means more to me than anybody in this whole world.

I don't have any inhibitions about going and talking to her, telling her how I feel or being moody around her, because she understands. And that's not how many people are today—understanding. After being really close for about a year, we haven't had one fight; and I've never had one bad thought about her. That's pretty fantastic. I've never once thought, *Oh, this or that about her bothers me.* She's the closest to perfect that I have ever known. Well, she has her flaws, but I can't think of any, off hand.

Sue and Jan would be good sisters because they're both so close to perfection: they always think of everybody else first.

Even if she's feeling down, Sue always has a smile. She's always got comforting words and knows the right ones to say. She's so strong—a shoulder to lean on—which I need sometimes.

And I repay her. She tells me what I consider to be privileged information, things that you wouldn't tell just anyone. I've always found it hard to keep a secret, but I can keep hers because I know she trusts me. And I trust her because I know she's not going to blab everything I tell her.

She has a life of her own, a busy person: cheerleading, a job, a boyfriend. But she's there to listen, even if I have to write her a note. Always there.

I'd like to be the sort of friend that you have been to me;
I'd like to be the help that you've been always
    glad to be;
I'd like to mean as much to you each minute of the day
As you have meant, old friend of mine, to me
    along the way.

I'd like to do the big things and the splendid things
    for you,
To brush the gray from out your skies and leave them
    only blue;

I'd like to say the kindly things that I so oft
    have heard,
And feel that I could rouse your soul the way that
    mine you've stirred.

I'd like to give you back the joy that you have given me,
Yet, the mere wishing you a need I hope will never be;
I'd like to make you feel as rich as I, who travel on
Undaunted in the darkest hours with you to lean upon.

I'm wishing at this Christmas time that I could but repay
A portion of the gladness that you've strewn along
    my way;
And could I have one wish this year, this only
    it would be:
I'd like to be the sort of friend that you have been
    to me.
                              Edgar A. Guest

    I have to go to bed 'cause it's late and I've had too many late nights.

    November 13. Oh, I have so much to tell, Phoebe. I don't even know where to begin. I've been feeling really down these past days. It's been a bad trip–you could say a bummer. I'm not really sure why, although I do have an idea: I feel like I'm ignored. I don't know if it's me or others, but I feel people are saying "Hi" because they have to. The only ones I don't feel are doing that are Sue and Lori. It's great having those two around. I don't know; I think it's me.

    Guess I'm still going through an identity crisis. I know who I am and what I want; but I'm not sure what others expect of me. Or, I know how I want to be, but I'm not sure how to become that person. That bothers me. Or, I know how I am and wish to change, but I can't . ;⌣

    Everybody around here has been bugging the heck out of me lately. They're getting on my nerves. I'm so sick of all the little cliques, being outside of it all. I don't have any close friends anymore, except Sue and Lori. I guess Sue will be in my writing lab, but Lori won't be in any of my classes. I don't know what I'm going to do when we switch terms, or next year when Lori leaves. We have so much fun together because we understand each other, have the same sense of humor. I just wish I had gotten to know her better before this year.

And I hate school. I wish I could leave and start over again, or just get out of high school and go to college. I know the responsibilities are greater and it's a bigger burden, but I just want out of there so badly. I want to go anywhere, to be by myself for awhile.

I tried to go to the movie tonight. First of all, I couldn't find anybody to go with, but I went anyway. All I'd taken was my driver's license and two dollars. When I got there, the movie was $2.50. I just said "Oh shit" and walked out. Two dollars and fifty cents! If I'd had it with me, I would have paid it. Since I couldn't, it made me mad.

Homecoming is over. Half the kids don't even date the ones they went with, but it was such a big deal! Really wasn't, but it seemed like it. All the people I know, or talk to, went; and I just feel so left out.

Last night when I was talking to Sue, I told her that there's one thing in my life that I want *now*. More than anything in the world. And she said, "A guy?"

And I said, "Yeah." I only wish there was somebody for me, somebody special—or even a lot of somebodies, not just one special guy.

Sort of fed up with everything right now. (Sigh) Wish I could go away. Turn into a hermit. Go to France and hibernate.

I am a hobo.
A tramp.
A bum.
A vagabond.
My food I beg for,
Search for,
Go without.
My home is the road,
Back alleys,
Deserted railroad tracks.

My roof is the sky.
My bed is the ground.
My friend is the outdoors,
And Freedom the law of my life. Lisa

November 29. Yesterday was Thanksgiving, so today was no school. I went to the first home basketball game, and afterwards to Diane's. Today I keep switching from good to depressed feelings. I didn't have friends to sit with at the game, but I got in a good mood at Di's. It was a small group so I mingled better. I'm insecure.

December 12. I wish the Christmas spirit would come; I don't feel anything yet. Once, when we were singing a carol and the organist was chiming, I felt the holiday glow; but it didn't stick.

Christmas will hold a note of sadness this year
Because five loved ones cannot be here.
But the Lord's birthday will be more glorious
Now that they are with Him at His celebrations.
Their smiles will fill the hearts of those who knew them,
With the joyous feeling of Love:
Love for those who are with us in body,
And for those who are with us in spirit.
Their memory will light the candle of Love:
Love for our friends,
Love for the world.
In the serenity and silence of Christmas Eve
And the gaiety of Christmas Day,
Their names will be remembered.
And, as I see their faces,
I will remember that this is a time of giving–
Because I will remember they gave me
Their gifts of love and friendship.
Christmas seems the time to remember
And to say, "I love you"
To Vida, Kim, Cindy, Holly and Evelyn.   From Lisa.

December 24. Tonight is Christmas Eve and I really cried. Singing "Silent Night" at the midnight church service and holding hands with my family in the darkness started my mood. I couldn't ever get into the spirit this year. The poem explains why: Five people I really loved have died this past year. Those guys are with Him, so it's really His celebration. I guess I feel sorry for their families. I feel *so* lucky.

Have a Merry Christmas, Phoebe! P. S. There is a Santa. His spirit is immortal.

December 26. I really thrive on the future and think about it constantly. I live for it; I don't live day by day. My plans include school, marriage, career and a long life. No kids–of my own, anyway.

These past few days I've been thinking about what it would be like to take a four or five-year-old and raise it–you know, without being married. I have a lot of love inside, and it's love I can't give to my family or friends. I need someone of my own to love.

Sometimes I think I'll go crazy. I've been so confused lately. Do you ever feel like you want the whole world to leave you alone? Or then for everyone to look at you and say, "Hello, Lisa"? YES. I feel like a nobody sometimes, a little particle that is taken for granted and goes unnoticed. I only hope I am someone to somebody. I don't want to leave this world without doing something that people will remember me by, will remember the way I've lived.

I've been discouraged and depressed a lot, too. God only knows why. I wish you could feel how I feel inside right now, Phoebe. I guess I feel trapped: I want my freedom. I want a lot of things that I'm not willing to work for. I'm tired of the same old routine at school; but I enjoy it, at the same time. I have a longing, this yearning for all that I want–and a need to be emotionally grown.

My most embarrassing moments stem from my tendency towards foot-in-the-mouth disease. If I would let things go at what I say, it would be OK; but in trying to cover up my blunder, I only succeed in stuffing my foot further down my throat. One episode still makes me cringe when I think about it.

Our school lockers are in rows, according to home-rooms. There was a Black girl, Wanda, whose locker was near mine. I was always messing around with her, teasing and giving her a hard time—only because she was so short.

One day when I was at my locker with another girl, Wanda came to hers. I put my arm out so she couldn't get by and said, "Say the magic password."

"What will you do if I don't?"

"I'll put you on my black list."

Her eyes grew enormously large and she just stood there, staring at me. The other girl left.

Realizing what I had said, I tried to make things better. "You can be on my white list, too."

"That's all right." And she went to her locker.

I just put my hands over my face, shut my locker door and left, too. If someone had laughed, it would have been better. No one did. Fortunately, she and I later became good friends.

You know, I'm two different people. On the inside, I'm brave yet weak, gentle, romantic and loving. On the outside, I'm sometimes sarcastic, strong and cold—afraid to be the "inside me." I wish I could combine them to be a strong and brave, gentle and romantic "outside-me."

> The lion's strength protects those weaker than himself,
> Like the gentle lamb
> Whose passiveness tames the king's power.
> Like the lion,
> We all have fierceness and strength;
> But it's the lamb's tenderness in us
> That softens our fierceness
> And makes us considerate
> Of others' weaknesses. Lisa

I wish I could be the ideal person that I'm not: Have fun; not be too straight or too crooked, someone that everyone would like.

I'm an idealist: I believe in the good in people, not the corrupt. I don't mind being extremely idealistic, but I wish I didn't judge people and things so often by hearsay—rumors and others' intuitions. I've got a mind of my own.

I want so much, and seem to get so little of what I dream.

Hold fast to dreams,
for if dreams die,
life is a broken-winged bird
that cannot fly. Langston Hughes

Last summer was the happiest I've ever been in my life. And I started this year with so much "pizzazz" inside. I want to get back and grasp firmly my zest for life again.

Life is so uncertain. I need things that are dependable. The world isn't like that, or I don't see it like that. I need a crutch to lean on that won't break under my weight.

Do you ever wish you could start all over again, Phoebe? Do everything you haven't done, enjoy what you want to, but don't? I wish I could. I want to forget that I have, or had, leukemia. Forget that I ever had to go to St. Jude. I could endure a lot of pain now, but I'm sick and tired of all the pain.

Do you know what it's like to go through life wondering if this cold, or if that bruise is a sign of relapse? It's an awful feeling. I don't think about it often, but it's always in the back of my mind.

I wish I lived in a book where I could write what would happen. I would know for sure what was on the next page, unlike life itself. I'm not a lover of surprises.

I'm never going to mention my leukemia again, except to those who know and care. When I go to college, no one but the infirmary is going to know. I'm tired of this business. SICK AND TIRED.

You know that saying, "Never put off till tomorrow what you can do today"? I'm not like that at all. I'm more like Scarlett O'Hara: "Tomorrow is another day." I know there'll always be a tomorrow—somewhere.

December 31. Looking back over the past year, I did a lot of growing, especially emotionally.

Of my last New Year's resolutions, I kept two: I kept this diary; kept my room *fairly* clean (1/2), and kept my temper down and smiles up (1/2).

Of eight things I wished to happen, only one came true: I stayed in remission. I wanted Evelyn to get well. She passed away, as did Cindy, Aunt Vida, Holly and Kim.

I celebrated three years of remission on April 23, my seventeenth birthday on October 25, and one year of no medications on November 27.

I had a fantastic summer: won a blue ribbon for my rhubarb pie at the All-Iowa Fair; went to Camp Highlands to visit Dana; wrote poems and revised my story; got my driver's license.

Had a rotten Christmas because I wasn't in the spirit.

Happy New Year! The world isn't going to get any better in 19–, but maybe my life will. It has to.

It was great knowing you, Old Year. I'm sorry you're leaving. I'll always remember you. Hang in there, Kid. Lots of love and kisses.

Happy New Year, Phoebe.

Dear Felicia

February 14. We are home now from another trip to Memphis. Not perfect, but OK. I'm probably relapsing slowly; they're surprised that I haven't yet. As long as I feel OK and there's no change.... Ten weeks again.

I'm frightened because both Cindy and Ginger are gone. We saw Paula and she's relapsed, but she gave me courage to say, "I've got a lot to do before I die, and I'm going to get it all done." I admire her courage.

This is courage: to remain
Brave and patient under pain;
Cool and calm and firm to stay
In the presence of dismay...

This is courage: to be true
To the best men see in you;
To remember, tempest-tossed,

57

Not to whimper, "All is lost!"
But to battle to the end
While you still have the strength to spend;
Not to cry that hope is gone
While you've life to carry on.

This is courage: to endure
Hurt and loss you cannot cure;
Patiently and undismayed,
Facing life still unafraid.... Edgar A. Guest (1881-1959)

I hope I win the fight, and I'm gonna put up a "biggy."
Hope I stay well through spring at least. I'm through sitting
around; I've places to go and things to do, Felicia.

Observantly down the trail we two filed.
Sandwiched between the snow, high-piled.
Thoughtfully each step was chosen,
While inside our boots, our toes were frozen.
The snow crunched silently beneath our feet,
Scarring the drifts with footprints neat.
All by ourselves we were that day,
Over drifts, carefully poking our way.
The sun burned brightly in the azure sky
As to the top we both drew nigh,
While 'round us the snow crystals whipped,
And melting icicles soundlessly dripped.
When we reached the top, we peered down below
At the powdered, ivory snow
As it glistened in the sunlight
Like many diamonds on a pillow white. Lisa

February 18. I've been changing moods so many times.
Saturday and Sunday I moped around feeling sorry for
myself, but then Sunday afternoon I snapped out of it. Today
I suddenly got depressed again. I think it was because I used
the busiest stairway at school, and I hate all the people
plowjocking into me.
      I have this urge to do EVERYTHING, and I want spring so

badly. Part of my problem is the winter blahs. I want to go bicycling and swimming, lie in green grass, smell lilacs and lilies of the valley, and become one with nature.

Snowflake
unique, delicate
floating, dancing, gliding
tripped by an eyelash
Snowflake.

Rain
melancholic, wet
dripping, drizzling, pouring
quenching the earth's thirst
Rain.

Music
discordant, enjoyable
floating, exciting, relaxing
for your listening pleasure
Music.

Spring
green, fresh
beginning, commencing, warming
clothing trees of winter
Spring. Lisa

I want to go to France. So much to do and so little time. If only there was no such thing as time.

I keep thinking of things to do with "my" (ha!) kids this summer. I want to be the best baby sitter they've ever had.

I want to meet new people and like them, get along with them. I want to have the best summer ever.

More than anything, I want to write. My poetry is ugh! and my prose isn't progressing any.

Fingers flitter through the dictionary until the wanted letter is seen. Deliberately now, they slowly turn the pages, eyes glued to guidewords at their top. The searched-for page is found, and my index finger trails slowly down a column, feeling each word as my eyes scan. They stop. The hunted is caught.

More than all else in the world, though, I want to leave a mark after I'm gone. I don't want to just live; I want to do something spectacular. And, God willing, I will.

February 21. It's almost March and still no sign of spring. I'm so sick of winter I could scream. I just sit around dreaming of grass, flowers and sun. Everything is reborn in spring, which always makes me feel so neat inside. I can run free with the wind and go barefoot through the grass.

I've been doing a lot of thinking lately, Felicia. You know, life is really very short; and it just doesn't seem long enough to do everything that I dream of. I'd like to go off to the woods for about a year and live without time–do the things I always say I'm going to, but put off for another day.

And if I didn't have to live with people, what I could do then! Like it or not, people are a hassle because you have to be pleasant and consider their feelings. I'm not down on the human race; it's just that I'm at a point where I need to get in touch with who I am and decide what I want out of life. I find that hard to do when surrounded by others who demand my time. I want my attention to focus undividedly on Life! True, people are a part of life and one must learn to cope with them; but I greatly fear for my dream world in which I like to live. My expectations become more and more discolored with each new experience I encounter.

For instance, I met a person who hated all non-Protestant religions–if you can believe that, Felicia–which adds up to 2,233,000,000 people, or roughly half the world's population! He also hated all Blacks. That is 296,147,000 people or 1/9 of the world's population. Quite a few people to dislike. Even more astounding is the fact that *this person doesn't know but a minute fraction of individuals from either of these groups!* There really are people like him, but it beats me how anyone can think this way.

Well, the sun is coming up over the horizon now and dawn is approaching, so I gotta go.

February 22. Brother, have I been in weird moods lately. I don't understand myself, so I don't think anyone else would either. Guess my emotions are growing and I'm just wrestling with them.

Last night at the game, I left at half time and sat in the car. I felt if I had to stay one more minute, I'd tear my hair out. I ran through all my thoughts, but still was in a rotten mood.

Wish there was no such thing as time: It's like sand slipping through our fingers. But there are beaches of sand; not so with time. You only go 'round once. Every grain of time should be admired and appreciated; we tend to take them for granted.

March 9. Have been a lot happier this past week. Don't know why, or what my problem was.

I love Clark Gable! Read his biography and saw a movie and TV special on him last night.

Old black and white reel-to-reels can't be beat.
The studio-owned stars,
With their fabricated life histories,
Were the greatest actors ever.
Never again will movies rise to such heights as
    they did in the
Thirties and Forties, before television.
Garbo, Crawford, Harlow, Loy,
Gable, Tracy, Laughton and the Barrymores—
Most are gone now,
But the screen will keep memories of them alive forever.

Lisa

Can't wait for summer: I dream about it all the time. Twelve days until spring.

March 22. Yesterday was the first day of spring. Nice! I'm in much better spirits lately—spring fever it's called. Am so excited about camp this summer, too.

March 24. As the days pass, an insatiable urge to be alone comes to me more and more often. I feel as if sociability is a noose tightening around my neck. People who once brought me joy now bring only annoyance and irritation. The senses of loneliness and aloneness have never been better defined to me than in these past months; and the majority of times when these feelings happen are generated by none other than myself. More and more I choose to be alone with my thoughts and my inner self than to be with the complaints and idiosyncrasies of others.

But am I content? No. I do as I please, only to remain unhappy. I love laughter and to make others laugh. Hard to do when I have secluded myself.

> Clowning around,
> The glad man of the circus
> Makes everyone happy.
> A sad, painted-on face
> Masks the laughter inside.
> The costume disguises the craziness
> That all of us possess,
> But are afraid to display.
> Making others laugh
> Is the clown's job,
> But also his joy. Lisa

I'm becoming expert at blocking out what I don't want to acknowledge. I can walk down the hall at school and not see anyone, or sit in a noisy room and hear nothing. The world could become a mess if everyone did that. Guess I'm trying to determine which I do want: people or myself. Someday my head will clear. Perhaps then I can reach a balance, delight again in the wonderment of others and the things they offer and can teach me. Maybe soon I will even figure out who I am and where I'm going. Now, however, I'd rather be alone with a good book, or be writing. I find I express myself better with paper and pencil than with other means of communications.

Mrs. King was a reproduction of a gracious hostess. In her imitation Parisian gown and rhinestone jewelry, she stood at the door of her rambling Victorian mansion, greeting dinner guests as they were chauffeured to the doorstep in long, black limousines. Her plastic smile welcomed all the town's socialites.

Old Mrs. King mingled about the room, her double chin wobbling as she absently chatted and laughed politely with her guests who were being served cocktails, dip and hors d'oeuvres.

Tasting some of the creamy dip, she noticed that the chopped pimientos were moving. With the aid of her lorgnette she discovered, to her horror, that the "pimientos" were red ants! She also saw that the dish was almost empty. A nightmarish vision formed in her mind: Seated at a table set with fine china and Bavarian crystal, her guests were talking about their children and discussing politics—with red ants crawling from their mouths.

"Agnes, dear, what's the matter? You look a little pale," fussed Rose, Mrs. King's closest friend.

"Wh–I–uh–why nothing, dear," she ducked. "I just need some fresh air. It's dreadfully warm in here. I think I'll step out on the terrace for a moment." With that, she fled to the patio to think of a solution.

A few minutes had passed when Rose joined her. Putting her arm lovingly around Mrs. King's shoulder, she murmured, "Agnes, dear, I'm not sure how to tell you this, but there are ants in your dip. Red ants! Wh–"

"Oh, I know." Mrs. King's unpremeditated interruption even surprised herself. "It's a recipe I picked up in the African jungles. Actually, it calls for black ants; but they're out of season, you know, so the cook substituted red ones. Do you think anyone will notice?"

Trying to hide her revulsion, Rose smiled weakly. "No, no dear. I don't think a soul will notice, if we don't tell them. Besides, the dip is gone now."

"Good," sighed Mrs. King, proud of her credible cover-up. "Let's go back inside before we're missed. It isn't good etiquette to leave your own party." With that self-reprimand and practiced grace, she entered the drawing room.

April 2. I can't believe it. April, and we have four inches of snow with more coming. I'm so sick of winter.

The twisted stump
Sits hunched and leafless
In our backyard.
Once it was young
And leafy.
It swayed in the breezes
And stood erect.
Now, its aged trunk
Huddles forward
Against the wind,
And its weak arms
Lie at its feet. Lisa

I think about religion more. I don't always show it, but I do believe. I read the Bible, pray, and really do have faith, Felicia.

April 8. Some days nothing I do seems to be good enough. If I settle for less than the best, I'm doing what I have hoped never to do: give up my goal to be the best that I can, or compromise my childhood dreams. My two greatest fears. Most people settle for less than they want, but I hope I'm never guilty of that. My goals may change, but God forbid that I should declare hopeless anything that I thought worthy of my time and efforts.

My career is most important to me, yet I want to explore emotional and spiritual things in life, too. I want experiences of knowing different cultures and seeing other places besides the good old USA. I want to travel to France, Canada, Switzerland, Monaco–anywhere that has French culture. That's my wildest aim: to meet people of all sorts, and to learn as much about them as my mind permits.

So you see, Felicia, I'm not going to settle for what I could have without work. I won't take what is handed me, and I don't want to settle for the easy life. I'll try for the next step higher and won't quit until I reach the top, whatever and wherever it may be.

April 17. I'm a little scared tonight. As my fourth anniversary draws near, I get more and more worried about my continued remission. A kid at school just found out he has leukemia, and we've been comparing notes. I'm not as confident as I appear to be.

I've been thinking. I'd like a husband, if I can find one that lives up to my ideals. I don't want any kids because I've seen too many parents lose theirs, to ever want to go through that with one of my own. Someday I might change my mind, but I doubt it.

I really enjoy my creative writing course. Poetry, too. Most of my writings are things that have happened to me or to someone I know.

Pets play an important role in the households of many families. Animals of all species can find homes where they will be loved and cared for. While some prefer the common cat or dog, or the no-fuss goldfish, there's a domestic or wild animal to fit everyone's personal taste for "creature comforts." Throughout the years, our family has had a wide variety of animals.

Our most unusual were a pair of ducks named Daisy and Donald that Dana, Ron and I raised from ducklings. Our church youth group had purchased the fowl to help teach responsibility to its members. Ours was the only family that favored such teaching aids.

An owner must adapt to his pet's habits and be governed accordingly. The first night with our three-week-old, feathered friends, we learned two things that became ironclad rules as long as they remained with us: First, it is dangerous to handle a duck without holding something under its tail; and second, setting a duck on unprotected carpeting results in a severe reprimand

and a job as carpet cleaner. Naively, we had thought that two such innocent looking babies couldn't do *all that!*

Giving one's pet a fine home of its own is important to raising a good-natured animal. Housing must be spacious and comfortable. Our ducks' first home was a large, cardboard box with luxurious, newsprint carpeting. When the ducks began to eat the walls of their house, it became necessary to move them into a roomier, wooden toy box.

Animals need to be kept clean and given access to their true surroundings. Every afternoon we bathed Donald and Daisy in the bathtub, but separately because we had only six hands. This ritual was like playing in a sprinkler-hose: Give a duck its natural habitat and it will show you its natural habits. After each daily swim/bath session, Mom made us scour the tub until the enamel began to wear off.

One must be willing to devote much time to the care and upkeep of a pet and its house. The ducks became our top priority–by necessity, not by choice. Because they are not members of the cleaner, animal species, it was necessary to haul their home outside, scrub and recarpet it *every day*. And try explaining to your friends, Felicia, that you can't come over now because you have to exercise the ducks.

Animals are creatures of habit. Once they have established a routine, the owner must observe their schedule. Our ducks' routines included a six o'clock walk around the block. Tamed birds need no leash, just a guide to waddle behind. Ours gawked at the people who lined porches along the street. They basked in admiring glances from the neighbors. The block came to know 6:00 p. m. as the duck, not the dinner, hour.

Most pets are capable of learning tricks; it takes patience to teach them each stunt. In our case, the ducks were self-taught. They had only one trick, but it wasn't one you would show off to your friends. While you were holding and talking to them, they would grab your lower lip in their bills and shake their heads from side to side. Their victim usually suffered a swollen, bloody lip–a painstaking trick.

Pets have idiosyncrasies too; an owner must adjust to and accept them. Ours were no exception, although their eccentricities were amusing. Donald was so pigeon-toed that he walked with one foot on top of the other. The poor thing waddled as it was, but his physical handicap pronounced it. Another extraordinary characteristic was that Donald actually was a "she" while Daisy was a "he."

The time comes when one must part with a pet, either because of its death or by giving it away. Having learned responsibility–mostly commanded by a higher-up–we, too, had to release our beloved ducks. We arranged a home for them at a nearby lagoon, but retained visiting rights. Later, their new owner told us that Donald had three ducklings; and he named Daisy as the father.

So, Felicia, if you can follow the requirements, you are ready for a pet. They are a lot of work, but bring life to your every day.

April 27. If ever there was a time to live each moment as if it were the last, it is now. As I slowly slip into relapse, I cherish each day more than the one before. So many burdens are placed on my back that I sometimes start to bow with their added weight.

Come, Courage, come, and take me by the hand!
I have a long and weary way to go,
And what may be the end I do not know–
I do not understand.

Come, Courage, come, and take me by the hand!
Be thou my mentor! Be my guide and stay!
The path is one I may not fare by day;
It leads through night's dim land.

Come, Courage, come, and take me by the hand!
Gird me with faith, the radiant faith to see
Beyond the darkness–immortality;
Thus may the gulf be spanned.

Come, Courage, come and take me by the hand!

Clinton Scollard (1860-1932)

At St. Jude this past weekend, the possibility of a bone marrow transplant was discussed. I'm very excited about it and wish they could go ahead and do it *tomorrow*. The chances of long term survival are much greater than with those having plain chemotherapy. I only hope and pray that one of my siblings is a match and will donate bone marrow. I'm very optimistic about one of them being able to be a donor because the chances are 1:4. With four siblings, I can't miss.

My only unhappiness is that I had to forfeit my summer employment at Camp Highlands. I had my heart set on that; it's a real disappointment. I have shed lots of tears; but if I'll be having a transplant instead, I won't mind half as much. But I'll still mind.

It's scary to think that I'm the only one of us four girls still in remission. Glenda now is in relapse so.... Someone is watching over and blessing me, but I'm afraid my time is running out, too.

My time has almost run out.
Very soon now I will be on my way to Heaven.
I have fought long and hard for my Lord,
And through it all I have kept true to Him.
Now the time has come for me to stop fighting and rest.

2 Timothy:4

If all fails, I've still had four years that a lot of people have never had. I thank God for those years. I still would like to graduate from high school and see France. If I have the transplant and it is successful, I will–God willing.

If you can only keep your chin up and smile at the clouds in the sky, you've run half the race with the wind at your back.

May the road rise up to meet you,
May the wind be always at your back;
May the sun shine warm upon your face,
And the rain fall soft upon your fields;
And until we meet again,
May God hold you in the palm of His hand. Irish Blessing

April 29. Linda and Dana flew in tonight so all of us can go to Iowa City to have our tissues typed. If there is a match, I'll go for the transplant. I'm terribly excited about the whole deal and wish to proceed immediately. I PRAY that there's a match. I was really upset that I can't go to camp; but if I'll be "cured," it's all right.

May 2. The waiting is almost unbearable. I say "almost" because if I'm busy with schoolwork, time doesn't exist. Actually, if I'm doing anything, I don't notice how fast or slowly time passes. I only hope I have enough to keep me busy tomorrow and Sunday.

I dream about what may happen, even when I catnap. The wildest possibility is that everyone matches. The idea of *not* having a match is so remote to me that I think I'll have a breakdown if there isn't one. I dreamed I was running and running–no match.

Help me to pass the time quickly.

May 5. The days drag on. We should know by tomorrow, for sure. Yesterday was my worst day. I left before the sermon and paced the corridors, hands clammy and clenched into fists. I was still so upset later, I couldn't even sew. I even cried. I snapped out of it, though, when I realized that worry makes time go slower and doesn't help at all anyway.

I never knew a night so black
Light failed to follow on its track.
I never knew a storm so gray
It failed to have its clearing day.
I never knew such bleak despair
That there was not a rift, somewhere.
I never knew an hour so drear
Love could not fill it full of cheer. John Kendrick Bangs (1862-1922)

It was so warm today. We went from winter to summer. The tulips are about gone, though still blooming. Violets appeared today; flowering almond last Saturday. I hope the lilacs bloom soon.

May 13. The waiting is finally over. Mom came to school at 11:15 a. m. and said Linda matched. She was crying, and we were hugging and kissing. Bet they all thought we were crazy.

We'll be going to Baltimore for 100 days! Linda won't be there more than ten days to two weeks. I'm a little scared, but more excited. I'll probably be really sick, and it is a hassle; but God willing, this is the answer to all our prayers. Thanks, for whatever....

May 14. Tonight I'm a little less excited about this whole thing. Don't misunderstand, Felicia. I'm not really scared about the transplant. I want to do it very much. I know that I've never been guaranteed anything, and they're not starting to do so now. It's just I'm a bit jittery now that plans are definitely shaping up.

Life! I know not what thou art,
But know that thou and I must part;
And when, or how, or where we met
I own to me's a secret yet.

Life! We've been long together,
Through pleasant and through cloudy weather;
'Tis hard to part when friends are dear—
Perhaps 'twill a sigh, a tear;

Then steal away, give little warning,
Choose thine own time;
Say not good night; but in some brighter clime
Bid me good morning. Anna Letitia Barbauld (1743-1825)

Being away from home and all my friends for three months is a long time. I've done it before; but that was long ago, and it wasn't easy then. What I dislike and what upsets me most is the fact that I'll probably lose my hair again. That is an appalling thing to happen to any teenage girl. If I was a guy, I could go "Kojak." I had a hair sample taken for another wig today.

I wonder how Linda feels. She doesn't have so much to worry about; but then, she's not used to being a patient, either.

Keep me steady and help me keep my chin up.

Faith:
If the wind is blowing in your face,
Turn around so it's at your back.

If it's raining on your side of the street,
Cross over to the other side.

If the load becomes too heavy,
Find someone to help you carry it.

If night comes early,
Go to bed, and get up with the sun.

If the sun goes into a cloud,
Wait. It has to come out the other end.

If you can't keep running,
Think, "Only one more step."

If all else fails,
Keep your chin up
And smile on.

Brighter skies are behind dark clouds. Lisa

May 18. Thursday I was really blue. I cried and called Sue. I cried some more; and when I was through, I was excited again. Wrecks the summer though. Everyone says I'll be fine. I believe them. It takes something like this to make you not take your health for granted. You have to follow the path to reach your destination.

May 25. I don't think I'm scared of dying anymore. Maybe I will be when they say, "You only have ten days to live." But I don't feel panicky when I think about it. That's good. I know there's a golden sunshine after this where it's spring all year, but I'm in no hurry to leave here.

Death:
Like a snake, coiled, waiting to spring on its prey,
Like a hidden pursuer in the night,
You wait to snatch me from the comforts I know.

Like a mother taking her child's hand,
Like a path to the mountain top,
You wait to lead me to the brighter world of Heaven. Lisa

The mountain stood in all its grandeur that early summer morning. A monument to nature, its weathered peak towered above the lake and cottages like a balding man who is already shiny on top and thinning on the sides. The trees became sparse on their way up the slope, until they disappeared completely and left a bare tip. All one hundred twelve Crayola colors could be found on the palette of the mountainside: Flowers polka dotted the green background. The tower of granite reigned in splendor over all.

Death comes to everyone some time. There isn't a "normal" time to die. The average age is in one's 70's, but I don't want to be "average." I want to be someone special. I hope I'll be remembered after I die.

I hope my writing, or some of it, will be published so I won't have lived in vain. It bothers me to think of all the people who have lived and now are just a name on a tombstone.

There are no lives unfinished, incomplete.
God gives each one at birth some work to do,
Some precious stone of strange, prismatic hue
To care and polish, till it shall be meet
To place with His temple, still and sweet.
'Ere that be done, the soul may not pass through
The door to grander worlds, to aim more true,
To wider life with love's sweet joy replete.
And if the working time be short, and earth
With its dear human ties be hard to leave,
Be sure that God who thought hath given thee
Still holds for the best thou canst receive;
Be sure the soul, in passing through that door,
Though losing much, gains infinitely more. Author Unknown.

I don't see how people can say, "Don't cry for me." When I die, I want them to cry. I can't lie about that. If they didn't, it would mean that I had lived without touching anyone; and I want to go, feeling as if I've contributed something to those with whom I've come in contact. I hope I've touched them with my love, given their lives something that wouldn't be, if I hadn't been a part of it. If no one mourned, I wouldn't be missed. Cry because you'll miss that certain something I gave you each day. Is that being selfish?

When someone I know dies, I cry. I'm happy to have been part of their lives. I cry not because I'm sad for them–that they died–but because I'll miss their smile, or their courage, or their inspiration.

Who could wish that someone keep suffering, for their sake? Wouldn't they rather be comforted by the person's dying than to have their presence to fuss over? Does that make any sense? I hope so.

Poem for the Living:
When I am dead,
Cry for me a little.
Think of me sometimes,
But not too much.
It is not good for you

Or your wife or your husband
Or your children
To allow your thoughts to dwell
Too long on the dead.
Think of me now and again
As I was in life
At some moment which it is pleasant to recall,
But not for long.
Leave me in peace
As I shall leave you, too, in peace.
While you live,
Let your thoughts be with the living. Theodora Kroeber

Sue and Michelle are my only friends who have seen my worst side. I don't like being ugly around people. I may not always smile; but I try to, and do, when I feel good. This summer I'm not going to cry at all. I hate self-pity, and I indulge in it too much.

What's there to feel sorry about? I'm going to have that "second chance" that so many don't have. I don't mind being sterile. I don't want kids—to give them life and wonder if they, too, will suffer. I've seen too many kids suffer.

It's strange how some people turn out. I approve of the way we were raised, with an iron hand and lots of love. But now that I'm seventeen—that sounds so mature, yet so young—I wish I had more freedom. I feel they still treat me like a child. I have common sense, and they taught me right from wrong. They have to trust my judgement. My beliefs and morals may differ, but they have to accept my views and have faith in what I do. Besides, some things you have to experience for yourself. No amount of preaching will make you believe differently until you have tried, and either failed or succeeded.

I'm not sure I'd know how to handle freedom and independence, if I did have them. I've been a "puppet" for too many, for too long. If I knew that what I must do depended solely upon my own self-discipline, I wouldn't put things off.

One thing that bothers me is the fact that I cover up how

I'm feeling with sarcastic remarks. I'm Lisa the joker. I never can say to most people what I really mean. I mask feelings with a put down. I wish I could say honestly what I'm thinking, unless it is bad. I hate hurting people and don't care for insensitive persons.

Two types I can't stand: The egotist and the prejudiced. Let that go down on record, Felicia. I hate those who constantly brag about themselves. Once in awhile is all right, but *all* the time? No! And those who think white is the preferred skin color are loony.

I don't gross out easily. In fact, I can't think of anything that makes me sick to my stomach–except the smell in a doctor's office and the idea of taking an ara-C shot again.

Few things scare me: thunder, window shades that snap up, mystery stories, weird bugs, being alone at night. Thunder is my greatest fear, I think; and it's completely harmless! I'll do almost anything that everyone else is afraid to do. Those who are scared disgust me, especially self-proclaimed, "masculine" men.

One thing that depresses me is that I'll go through life, however long or short, without being loved by and loving in return–a man, that is. I fear terribly that my disease, even if it no longer were there, will always be a barrier. If someone couldn't love me because of it, granted, they aren't worth loving. In true love, that shouldn't matter. It would be a "fault." But I think men will say, "I want a perfectly healthy woman."

I'm so idealistic. I think that's why I love to read–to romanticize about life. If I could have a man with as much love for me as Rhett had for Scarlett, my life would be heaven. But is such a thing possible? I want a love that would never stop growing. Can it be? I have so much to give. If the right man would come along, I could burst. But here my idealism hurts me: I don't know if anyone will ever live up to my standards.

If a genie popped out of a lantern right now and said I could have three wishes, one would be to go to France. If I could go there, I'd be the happiest girl in the world. What's more, I might not come back: I might find a sexy Frenchman. Ha! ☺

If I could try three new things, they would be (1) hang gliding, (2) sky diving and (3) flying (as a) pilot.

I can't believe how much I've come out of my shell these past two years. Before, I was always so agreeable, noncommittal, bashful. Now, I figure if others say and do as they feel, so can I. No one can punish me for doing and saying what I believe. Right, Felicia? Sometimes, though, I feel like I can't do anything right. I'm prone to depression spells; but when I think about how much I have and how lucky I am, I cheer up again.

God, I hope I'm courageous when I die, not whining and whimpering with complaints. I'd like a certain amount of attention, but I never want to be burdensome. I hope I die quickly, without lingering or suffering. I don't want machines or drugs to prolong my life. If I'm really going to die, I want to go naturally, with just something to ease the pain. I want to die smiling, an inspiration to others. That's how I want people to remember me.

Somewhere between comics and classics,
I lost my childhood.
Someplace betwixt my diary and my room,
I found myself. Lisa

June 1. Well, we're on our way! After a tearful farewell with the family and Sue, we hit the road. I feel like I should be scared, but I'm really not. I'm just enjoying my last days of freedom before being holed up on Tuesday. We should be in Baltimore tomorrow afternoon. I'm already sick of riding in the car!

Last night Grandma and Ron's girlfriend, Charlotte, came for dinner. Charlotte made one of her fabulous cakes, chocolate with green and white frosting, in the shape of a horseshoe. The icing writing said "Good Luck, Little Stinker" and there was a ceramic skunk on top. I brought him with me for good luck.

Even though I know I'll be sick, I can't think that anything is going to be too terrible. I've been through a lot and can't imagine much worse. I may be mistaken. But three things still upset me: losing my hair, missing camp and fishing and the sun, and being away so long. September sounds *so* far away.

June 2. Well, we're all here in Baltimore now. Linda flew from Minneapolis. I fell in love with Pennsylvania; it's so green and hilly. Beautiful! This was my last day of freedom and I spent most of it in the car. ⁀ii⁀

I have a slightly sore throat today; neck's a little swollen. I have a feeling my remission has ended. Don't know, though. Better get some sleep. Still not nervous. *Pray.*

I told Mom that I had something I wanted to say tonight about all this. I said that *I* was planning to have this work done so I could get all well and go home again. But that I knew it may not be, and that I may die here. She must know that I *wanted* to come. It was my own decision to have this transplant. I don't want to die; I want to live. But no matter what happens, either way, it's all right. I wanted her to know that. I also said in case it doesn't work out right, I have left some funeral plans in a metal box on my dresser at home. Then I asked her not to mention this to me again.

June 3. Today was a lot of waiting and preliminary stuff. I was ready to cry when I saw my room: small and no TV. But things started looking up when they brought one in, and I made the room more homey with my junk from home. They can't believe I'm the patient because I look so healthy. Guess I'll get some sleep. A. M. comes early in the hospital.

June 4. Today was worse than yesterday. I shouldn't complain; Linda had it all, too, except for a bone marrow test. I started to cry once, but only a tear or two escaped. I fought them off. This is probably fun compared to what will happen.

I got back my own pillow. Mom didn't think I could have it in isolation; but when we asked the doctor, he said, "Sure."

I feel like a big pin cushion. Nothing on me hasn't been

poked, pushed, prodded, jabbed, punched, hit, felt, squeezed, looked at, looked in or kneaded. I feel as if I'm on display. The people are all nice, friendly and honest, so I don't mind as much.

June 12

Dear Lin,

Thank you for your bone marrow. Hurry and come down to see me. Enjoy the flowers since I can't.

I love you.
Lisa

June 13

Dear Lin,

Good morning! Hope you feel better today. I've had a bath, sat up, and brushed my teeth. ☺ Come see me later.

I love you,
Lisa XOXO

Hi!
I'm bored so I'm writing you a note. How are your hips? Do you feel better? I'm going to watch some T.V. tonite, I think. If you get in a wheel chair come see me. I love you. Lisa

June 16. (letter to a friend) Hi! from the big city of Baltimore. Note the change of address on the envelope.

Well, I'll start from Sunday, June 1, when we left. We stayed all night in Ohio, and arrived here Monday around 3:00 p. m. I fell in love with Pennsylvania: I'm going to move there! We picked up Linda at the airport that evening.

Tuesday I was admitted. Gobs of usual tests. The nurses asked me what the diagnosis was, and I said AML. She asked when it was made; and when I said more than four years ago, she looked real funny. Later, she called Dad out in the hall to see if she'd heard right. She was even more shocked when I told her I felt fine and wasn't on any meds. The staff didn't even know which of us was the patient, Linda or me. We had a laugh over that.

Wednesday was more tests and I went into protective isolation. I could walk around with a mask.

Thursday I had a bone marrow, and Lin and I both had skin tests.

Friday I had a lumbar puncture and a shot of methatrexate in my spine in case any leukemic cells got in during the procedure. Had a *terrific* headache from it. Also had two units of Lin's blood. $\overset{\frown}{+\!+}$

Saturday they started four days of Cytoxin, and I was pretty ill and sedated those days.

Wednesday was my day of rest and I moved to the laminar-flow room.*

Thursday Lin went to surgery from 8:00 to 10:00 and had sixteen aspirations. She yielded 410 cc. of marrow. The quantity was less than they like; but quality was better, so the yield was good. She's so little–5'0" and 88 lbs. No one could believe she was 25 years old and married. She and her husband left yesterday. That was sad.

So now, every other day I get a small dose of Cytoxin, for a total of five. Yesterday was #2.

Mom and Dad are staying at the nurses' residence. She's on the 4th floor and he's on the 9th. Cozy, huh?

They have weird eating hours here: continental breakfast at 7:30 a. m.; brunch at 11:00, with stuff like chili and goulash; supper at 4:00 p. m. and snack at 7:30. I'm hungry when there's no food and not when there is.

I feel fine and find all this to be interesting and exciting. I have no apprehensions and little fear. Everything has turned out before. This will too!

Hi! and Love to All. Please Write.

After Death:
The clouds part
And the storm breaks up,
The wreckage lingering in its aftermath.

The rain ceases,
But the sun is slow to reappear;
Its rays are weak, at first.

---

*The laminar-flow room funnels sterile air into the room at the patient's head of the bed area and circulates it in a clockwise direction in order to provide a bacteria-free environment.

As the light grows stronger,
The water evaporates.
Patches of wet sidewalk are a reminder of
    the passing storm.

Activities recommence. Lisa

    I can't imagine leaving Earth without leaving something
of myself here for other people. Writing comes so naturally; I
wonder what it would be like to be unable to express myself
through words, verbally or written.
    I have a picture of Mom reading my journals and poetry
after I die. It will be like me being there with her, talking to
her, because everything I write is something I feel or have
experienced.
    Sometimes I wish I could sing or draw; but writing is my
music and what I write, my picture.

A
star
shone
in the sky.
Twinkling ☆ it winked at
the half moon and
it shook hands
with its
point.
☆
Lisa
☆

Remembering

Sometimes one recalls small events as readily as momentous ones. Memories of these incidents are to our lives like the tiny scratches on fine silver that accumulate from use, enhance its beauty, and give it depth and patina.

Persons also enrich us with their example and words, grand or humble. In this context, I have added to Lisa's story some of my rememberings of her, my fourth child, and of her life before and after the diagnosis of terminal illness.

Lisa Virginia Pugh arrived at 6:44 one Friday evening after a long and difficult labor because, as the doctor described, "She chose to enter the world looking at the ceiling instead of the floor." Her complexion was smooth and rather dark. She was not fat, but a solid, little chunk of child. Thin, straight, light brown hair was difficult to manage most of her life. Once, when she was a baby, I tried to style it for a photograph with a large curl on top of her head; but dozens of hairs popped out in unruly wisps. After Lisa became bald from chemotherapy, she rejoiced when it grew back thick, darker brown and curly. Something good in everything, she observed. Her most outstanding feature was her eyes–large, dancing, hazel eyes with long, curly lashes. I can close my own and visualize them still.

Lisa walked quite early and was a climber: on top of the piano, on top of the refrigerator, over the sides of the playpen and crib. If it could be climbed, she mastered it. Although an active toddler, she was not very mischievous.

A determined and sometimes temperamental child, she had tantrums until age three or four. I would confine her to her bedroom where she would kick and scream and scream and kick, without shoes so she could not destroy the paint. Afterward, she would become quiet and emerge, ready to rejoin society and full of smiles as if nothing at all had happened.

I soon saw that Lisa was not a negative person. When she was about three, we forgot her at church one Sunday. Already at home, we counted and realized she was missing. When we returned, she was calmly standing by the door. Faith that we would come back had held her by the hand, not fear.

From the beginning, Lisa was a shadow of her sister, Dana. One of their favorite pastimes was to play "booty parlor" in the living room—combing, curling and designing hairdos for any willing, patient subject. Although sixteen months younger, Lisa tended to be the leader. Dana would not go to the tot lot playground in the summer until Lisa was old enough; and she would not attend camp until Lisa could, too.

When Dana went to kindergarten, it was a tearful crisis: Dana would walk down the street crying because Lisa could not go, while Lisa would stand crying on the front porch because she had to stay home. Several weeks passed before the two adjusted to being apart. Even then, Lisa would sit on the porch on the Wonder Horse, rocking as hard as she could, watching for Dana. Since we lived across the street from the school, a teacher said that she could see Lisa and often thought she might rock right off the porch, or at least tip over; but she never did.

The girls used to serve me breakfast in bed on Mother's Day. One year it came with a menu—of mostly misspelled words. After our first homecoming from St. Jude, Lisa brought breakfast to me, as usual, even though she was scarcely strong enough to walk alone.

Their older brother, Ron, loved to tease the girls, to make them squeal and tattle. He would stare fixedly at them during meals, which Dana ignored but which caused Lisa to fly into a tizzy and holler, "Mom, Ron is *looking* at me." Yet, she developed a quick, subtle sense of humor, perhaps a partial result of having siblings who liked to clown.

I remember the day Lisa started kindergarten. She went to our front door and said, "You don't need to go. I can go by myself." Although I did walk with her to the building, she went in alone. Little did I realize how much she would need that independence later, or how many doors she would have to walk through alone. At times I was concerned how to guide so much self-sufficiency without stifling it. I really had no cause to worry: her ideals and goals moved her only in directions that she considered worthy of time and effort.

At the first conference, I wondered just what I would hear because so often she came from school erupting with frustration, or enthusiasm. When the teacher commented about "that sweet, little Lisa," I laughed and replied, "You must have the wrong child."

According to her, Lisa was a model child, a behavior that was observable in all situations outside the home: spunky, but tempered by a desire to cooperate, to please, and to accept others as they were. I soon realized that she needed space at home in which to explode *because* she was so "perfect" elsewhere.

As number four of five children, a special treat was to visit her grandparents who lived nearby and who would take them, one at a time, to spend a weekend. Lisa was elated when it was her turn for undivided attention. When her grandfather died soon after our first trip to St. Jude, Lisa had much difficulty accepting his death.

Basically, she was quite healthy, with few problems before leukemia: occasional ear aches, tonsillitis, corrective shoes for a time to amend "toeing in," a single suture on her head from an accident on the backyard swing set, and a dislocated finger from a failed handspring.

Because she became a bit chubby in the sixth grade, she was not bothered when she first lost so many pounds from her illness. It was great to be slim, in fact. But as the weight drop continued, finally to eighty pounds, the novelty wore off. She regained to one hundred pounds about a year after the diagnosis, yet never maintained a steady weight until she went off medications. Then she stabilized at 115 pounds, with conscious dieting so as not to "get fat" again.

Another striking feature was Lisa's hands–tapered, with long fingers. She let the nails grow to accent their length. I liked to watch her write with those slim, graceful hands, probably because I did not admire my own boxy ones with their large, ugly knuckles.

From the time Lisa began school, she was an excellent student, although she glossed over academic honors. She was an avid book listener when young, and a "reader" long before she learned how. Fascinated with words, she kept a card file of new ones and their definitions, and made a point of using them in conversation or in writing until they became natural to her vocabulary. She also liked to baffle others with words unknown to them–sort of a private game.

Wherever she was, Lisa loved being part of the group– neighborhood playmates, Camp Fire, church, school, choir. While she conformed well, she did not always follow the crowd, even in her teens. She could be congenial without yielding to consensus. When she was occasionally excluded from a party after her illness, she felt deeply hurt; but most of her friends overextended themselves to include her because they knew how much being "one of the gang" meant.

Michelle was a close, neighborhood friend. Just before Lisa was diagnosed, the two had been working on a hide-away in the loft of Michelle's parents' garage. The girls carried heavy, upholstered furniture up the stairs. When Lisa showed a few bruises, we thought them caused by their labors.

Michelle stopped after school to learn why Lisa had been absent on the day we received confirmation of her disease. On hearing the sad news, they looked up "leukemia" in the encyclopedia. It reported incorrectly that the disease is always fatal. The girls simply sat and looked at each other. Neither knew what to say. Then Michelle got up and went home.

The two remained close friends even after Michelle moved to the St. Louis area. Once she accompanied us to St. Jude for a clinic visit, and we usually stopped to see or to phone her when traveling to or from Memphis. She was a valued support person for Lisa.

It seemed a happy coincidence that our only dog, a little, black, poodle puppy, was purchased just prior to the onset of Lisa's illness. Peppi, too, became a devoted companion when she had to be at home or confined to bed. Ironically, she also lived to be nearly seventeen.

But a live pet could not go to the hospital, so Lisa accumulated a stuffed menagerie: a large giraffe named *Blevrdmp*, a tag concocted from the first name initials of our family; Ralph Ray, a well-worn teddy bear from infancy who slept with her at St. Jude and went on all trips to X-ray; a tiny, white bear–made for her by Dana–that slept bedside in a facial tissue box; a ceramic skunk-a good luck token; and another favorite, a dog made of real fur, which had to be rescued from our pet when we came home. Peppi attacked her rival, either in a jealous rage or a territorial "fight," and bit out a chunk of fur.

Lisa enjoyed cooking and sewing. Unknown to us, one year she entered a rhubarb pie in the All-Iowa Fair. It was a beauty. Even more amazing, she won a blue ribbon with this first attempt. Later, she baked another for a favored inhalation therapist at St. Jude. She made most of her own clothes and was buried in a pale blue and white outfit that she had sewn.

Certainly Lisa was the person she was, at least in part, because she had leukemia. Happiness came to her in small packages–like a horseback ride in the country, a picnic with a French "flavor," or a weekend at college with Dana to sample dormitory and campus life. She spent much time with books and writing because she lacked physical energy for other activities. She thought about illness and dying because she was facing them. Since normal, more carefree teen years were denied her, she tried to accept and live life as it was offered.

From the first, the diagnosis of acute myelocytic leukemia meant that Lisa's chances of going into remission were about twenty percent. Until we arrived outside St. Jude hospital, though, the situation seemed to me like a bad dream. But there we were, and this was reality. I remember stepping down from the shuttle bus and thinking, *I simply cannot walk into that building.* Yet, I knew I had to. I looked at that huge statue of St. Jude Thaddeus, patron saint of the hopeless, that then stood in front of the hospital. It seemed like a large, white angel, keeping watch. Oh, how we were going to need his blessing!

A team of physicians worked with Lisa: Dr. A– from Brazil, a doctor from the Philippine Islands, and a third one from Chile. Lisa loved each, but seemed especially drawn to Dr. A– because he was such a gentle, caring person. I will always remember his first talk with us. Tearfully, he admitted, "The hardest part of my job is telling the parents." He added that he did not want to imply there was no hope because "there is always hope."

We signed the first papers giving permission for treatment, an exercise that would be repeated time and again. The medical personnel were diligent in explaining possible side effects which could range from mild to severe. Since chemotherapy was her only life-saver, we really had no choice. Lisa was to receive Azauridine intravenously, and daily, for ten times; Mercaptopurine daily; and Vincristine weekly for a total of four to eight doses, dependent upon her progress.

By evening of the first day of treatment, Lisa experienced mild nausea which soon afterward changed to "extreme," and was accompanied by chest pains. Subsequent days blurred as she struggled to retain vital liquids to avoid dehydration and grappled with the first bouts of homesickness. She also received several transfusions of packed, red cells and platelets; but the cards and gifts that already were arriving from family and friends seemed just as curative.

Gene and I were housed at the Medicenter, a long-term recuperation facility, then managed by a well-known, motel chain. The fifth floor was assigned to St. Jude families and patients, many of whom had to live there for several weeks as outpatients taking radiation. We could be with Lisa from noon to 9:00 p. m. daily, with free transportation between the hospital and living quarters.

During our stay, we discovered there were no charges at St. Jude, a fact of which we had been unaware when we were referred. The staff said they hoped people chose the institution because it was the best place for treatment. Certainly that was our reason, but it was a pleasant surprise to learn that the hospital did not then even have a billing department!

In early April, Gene flew home. Although we had kept in touch with the family by telephone, we felt he should be with the three children still living at home and should return to work. Linda, our oldest daughter, already had completed her education, worked as a medical secretary and lived in her own apartment.

At age seventeen, Lisa's brother, Ron, became the head and backbone of the family at home. Such a responsibility to serve as a substitute parent, when both were away, when one is a high school senior. But each of us had to adjust to a difficult situation, and did.

Dana, our ninth-grader, became cook, laundress and cleaning lady at age fourteen. She kept the household routine running smoothly, but not without learning experiences—like the time she changed the linens from five beds and proceeded to wash all ten sheets in one load!

Mark was our youngest, an eleven-year-old fifth grade student. I am sure the whole situation was hardest for him to comprehend. He developed enormous independence; but, at the same time, leaned heavily on others for his needs and support. Relatives, neighbors and friends made what seemed an impossible situation possible for the Pughs.

Pain in Lisa's back, hips, chest and stomach became so intense during chemotherapy that morphine had to be administered intravenously, an amount that was increased when an abdominal infection raged later. She developed double vision and floating spots in one eye. Neither of us would ever forget her withdrawal: nightmares, hallucinations, screams about spiders in her hair, birds attacking her eyes, and about being locked away—horrors of all sorts. In the years of remission, she vigorously would express contempt and abhorrence for the misuse of drugs.

For the next few weeks, our hopes vacillated constantly according to Lisa's condition. Vincristine apparently caused her severe nausea and pain, but frequent infections necessitated other unsettling medications and red cell transfusions.

When the mouse visited Lisa's room, the incident became more emotionally stressful for me than it did for her. Because I already had left for the night and was unaware of their moving her to another room, I was unprepared next morning. I went to her room. It was empty. Knowing what that usually meant, my heart dropped clear to my shoes. I just stood, not wanting to ask questions. A nurse came by, immediately surmised my thoughts and explained. But I had felt terror.

Student nurses were assigned to assist with patients on a one-to-one basis and to work in the outpatient clinic. One of them and I bathed Lisa, changed her bed and brushed her hair, which had not been tended for days while she was so sick. It came out by handfuls, a terrible blow to her. Many did not lose hair from Vincristine; but she did, practically every one. Lisa became so fond of this student that she kept contact by correspondence and in return visits. The student, on the other hand, was so influenced by Lisa that eventually she became a Hospice nurse.

Otherwise, she was improved; and a month from her admission, Lisa was in remission. She celebrated with Sugar Smacks, soda crackers and Hi-C! The following three months, however, were not easy rowing for any of us.

Mononucleosis developed, with its attendant complications. A second, mysterious virus accompanied by high fevers and water retention attacked after that, and remained undiagnosable. Gene was home when the doctor told me that "things could go either way." Every medication or procedure which might help had been exhausted. There was nothing more; it was wait-and-see, without a predictable outcome.

With this news, I went to the Medicenter and cried for two hours straight. Then I showered and returned to spend the night in vigil.

Since Lisa could not survive another such illness, we stayed in Memphis until her splenectomy, then an experimental, research protocol. Past experience had led physicians to believe that a malfunction of the spleen somehow was tied into relapse of patients with myelocytic leukemia. Lisa made a remarkable recovery from the surgery, except for another unexplained fever that detained her an extra week.

Part one, the in-hospital treatment was concluded; part two began in-clinic, with her as an outpatient.

School started the end of August and Lisa was there, although quite fragile. I worried so much that she would be bumped on the stairs, or be pushed and fall. Determination paid off, again. In her eyes, attendance was a struggle, but imperative.

As I write this, so many memories flood over me–some hurtful, others painless. I suspect it shall always be. There were many good times, and exciting ones, when each small step of progress seemed a miracle; and we knew it. Some events have faded from recollection, but not the people. My heart still aches for those whom we knew who lost the fight during those first four months. There were successes, too, who continued to be well, the last we knew. When one lost, everyone lost. When someone conquered, everyone was a winner.

Lisa spent the rest of her life in a dying-renewing microcosm. She usually met it with courage, happiness and a willingness to risk, again and again. She did not begin with these attributes.

At first, she would cry, feeling so overwhelmed by it all. The personnel at St. Jude did well in treating the whole person because certainly one's emotional and psychological development are as important as medicine to one's physical gains. Lisa developed a positive attitude about her illness and prognosis, but not without doubts along the way.

During the first weeks, she would ask, "Why? What have I done that God would do this to me?" We tried to convince her that this was not His punishment; that no one knew the cause of leukemia, but that an answer would be found, one day.

Eventually, Lisa found her own answers. She identified stages of her illness as she saw them: disbelief, anger, acceptance. All could be observed, the latter through expression of her faith in God's goodness, reasserted in her life and writing. Also, when remission appeared to be slipping from her and the decision was made for a bone marrow transplant, Lisa asked her brother-in-law to document her coming experiences with photographs. She felt that a visual record might be of assistance in the research of myelocytic leukemia. Whether or not she triumphed personally, Lisa wanted to help.

I remember one particularly traumatic time. We had arrived about midnight at St. Jude. Lisa was seriously ill. She was diagnosed with pneumocystis pneumonia, a dreaded word throughout the hospital. The survival rate at that time was about twenty per cent. In fact, more leukemic children died from this disease than from their cancer.

I sat by Lisa's bed, my head resting on the mattress. She had had a battery of tests and was hooked to oxygen, IV's–the whole works. I was devastated. I will never forget the nurse who assessed the situation when she entered the room, hugged me and then procured a cot so I could sleep the night beside Lisa.

These three weeks were perilous; and the attack possibly caused later repercussions–the real culprit that precipitated pneumonia when she was at Johns Hopkins. No one ever knew for certain.

One of Lisa's first physicians, however, was instrumental in developing a vaccine that is without side effects and totally effective against this type pneumonia. So, it no longer is a problem for patients with leukemia.

When Marlo Thomas visited St. Jude hospital, it was a thrill. Because Lisa was in isolation, Marlo could not enter her room; but she talked from the doorway and waved as she passed by. During a later, clinic appointment, Lisa had her picture taken with Danny Thomas. Afterward, she wrote him and received a personal reply. Special attentions boosted morale.

The most memorable of all days, though, was when the medications for the four girls undergoing the same treatment were stopped. Everyone knew there were a multitude of risks, but one cannot imagine the euphoria when the chemotherapy and especially *The Shot* were no longer a part of our lives. Unfortunately, because the film processor spoiled Gene's snapshots, we have but one picture of this landmark event, which the hospital had made for its permanent files. Back at home, though, Lisa had a "Going Off Meds" party at which she commented that no one, except one who also had been released from the treatment, could possibly understand how big the celebration actually was; but pictures from that event caught the feelings.

I remember a funny incident that Lisa never let me forget. She had wanted to have her ears pierced. Fearing infection, I refused. During a clinic visit, she asked Dr. Simone if she could have the procedure. He thought it a fine idea and offered to do it for her, if she would bring 14k. gold posts to her next checkup. Whereupon, Lisa chortled, opened her purse and produced the posts for his promised deed.

During one regular clinic call, Lisa thought it pretty

clever to turn the tables on Dr. Simone when she visited him while he was a patient. She threatened him with a joke, but heeded his plea for mercy because it was so soon after his surgery.

Physicians must maintain objectivity and professionalism; but we saw many instances of personal involvement, perhaps more likely with long-term patients. On Lisa's four-year remission anniversary, our local doctor sent her a bouquet of one dozen, long-stemmed roses.

News of the first questionable cells that signaled the beginning of relapse was a bleak moment for everyone. Once, Lisa just sat down on the kitchen floor and sobbed uncontrollably. Fortunately, Gene was at home that day. The two cradled their grief together and emerged with greater understanding, acceptance and a renewed determination to maintain hope.

The most nerve-racking time occurred as we awaited results from the tissue typing for Lisa's bone marrow transplant. The entire family had been tested on April 30, but results were not forthcoming until May 13. Then, additional testing delayed the "go ahead" until May 23. The procedure was another huge risk; it also was Lisa's last chance. With every phone call we thought, *This is it.* If there were no donor match.... I cannot describe the waiting.

At the onset of discussion about the transplant, we did not even know where it might take place; for St. Jude was not then equipped for the technique. In May we were informed that Johns Hopkins in Baltimore was our destination and that a pioneer in the field was to be Lisa's primary physician. Subsequently, we talked twice by telephone with him. He cautioned that the success rate was only fifteen to twenty percent; but this figure doubtless was higher than the one for myelocytic leukemia. The prognosis was not promising. It was better than nothing.

Since the doctor was concerned about our driving, rather than flying, to Maryland, Lisa had to have additional blood work, which postponed departure until May 23. Results from the platelet count were satisfactory enough; white cells of the type that fight infection were zero. While there was no dramatic change in her clinical condition, reports would show that she was admitted to Johns Hopkins with leukemia cells in the blood and bone marrow.

In the motel the night before admittance, Lisa suddenly sat down on the bed and shared her feelings and funeral plans with me, "in case it doesn't work out." So often in the night I still can hear her say, "It's all right." Looking back, I cannot comprehend her faith and courage at this moment. I cannot really know how it feels to be seventeen years old, full of dreams and plans, yet know that death may be just around the corner.

June 12 was *Transplant Day!* Her physician reported that bone marrow and biopsy tests were good: "As of today, things couldn't look better."

The full impact of this medical course hit me when Linda returned from surgery. As Dr. Simone had said at St. Jude, "Statistics don't mean a thing to you at this point. It is 100% or nothing." Suddenly I realized that we were participating in a drama, not reviewing it like a story in some magazine. Lisa's life was at stake. This *was* all or nothing.

Linda was released, very sore, but otherwise fine. Lisa was most homesick that weekend. She cried and cried to go home.

"Ask them if I can go. I won't stay. I'll come back; but, please, let me go home for just one day."

This was the only time while we were in Baltimore that she cried. Afterward, she was ashamed. I assured her that there was nothing to be ashamed about, that crying helps us to feel better sometimes, and that she had good reason to cry.

"No," she replied. "I had decided that I wasn't going to cry all summer, no matter what happened. I'm ashamed that I broke my promise to myself."

The next few days were routine. She received small doses of Cytoxin, antibiotics, and platelet transfusions. When we received a letter telling that a third girl of the original four had died about five weeks after relapse, we knew the right, and only, decision had been made in Lisa's case.

Then, several symptoms appeared concurrently: one drug caused fevers that peaked at 107 degrees; the bed would rattle from her uncontrollable shaking; she needed daily transfusions of platelets, red and white cells; she developed potassium deficiency, routine with transplants, and fluid retention.

About June 25, Lisa began significant improvement; and bone marrow tests looked encouraging for "a take," a successful operation and the subsequent production of her own healthy, white cells. She wanted pizza and red licorice! She got them.

Gene went home on June 30 and Lisa emerged from isolation July 2. I shall never forget the day. When I arrived at the hospital, she was sitting in a wheelchair by the desk, where I would be certain to see her as soon as I got off the elevator. By evening, she was running a fever and problems were compounding again: water retention, questionable lung congestion, low blood gases–all of which accelerated during the next four days.

Now she required an oxygen mask. Thus, time passed–one hour a little better, the next a bit worse. By the evening of July 9 when she began to spit up blood, I called for Gene to return.

Again the doctors could not promise she would even survive the night. Another permission paper to sign for yet another examination, a bronchoscopy, the only method to learn the cause of the bleeding. Lesions in the lungs could be treated. Diffuse bleeding signaled a critical condition.

Afterward, Lisa said, "Don't you ever let them do that to me again." The look on her face nearly broke my heart. She insisted upon hearing the results: There was diffusion in both lungs, but not as extensive as they believed it might be. A grim outlook, nonetheless.

Gene called back, deeply distressed and frustrated: he was unable to get flight connections until the following day.

Lisa received nine bags of platelets and two of red cells as rapidly as could be administered. If she were to hemorrhage severely, there was nothing they could do. All night I sat by her bed. That was all I could do for her.

I had "bottomed out" when the bronchoscopy was ordered because they had informed me that even the examination could cause a fatal hemorrhage. Now, with bleeding in both lungs, I was too numb to cry. "Devastated" doesn't even begin to describe what I felt, but I did feel very alone.

By some miracle, Lisa improved again. Bleeding stopped and breathing stabilized by the following evening. I had told her primary physician the night before that if no other means could help, she and we, her parents, did not want "heroic measures" to keep her alive with machines. I will always remember his answer. "The patient comes before research."

Once again, conditions indicated a successful transplant. Steady or slight improvements were read on the charts for the next couple of days. While transfusions of platelets, red cells, plasma, as well as white cells from Gene to fight infection were often standard fare, Lisa relished a popsicle!

By the night of July 13, she was miserable. Except when she had been heavily sedated or when she had morphine withdrawal, this was the only time in which her mind was not clear. Later, I realized she was not getting enough oxygen to the brain. Her thoughts wandered from one subject to another, but all from her past. She believed she was home and called for our family doctor. She wanted an egg, but not to eat; and I could not learn for what reason. She went through complete motions for making a rhubarb pie. She talked about Barbara, her imaginary friend. I stayed the night.

The next morning, July 14, just after I told her that I was leaving to get some rest and that her Dad would soon be there to stay with her, Lisa spoke her last words to me. "Oh, Mom, I am so sick."

I replied that I knew she was; that the doctors were doing

everything possible to help; that she should just hang on and let us take care of her.

She took my hand and said, "I love you, Mom. I love you so much. You know, people just don't say that to each other often enough."

When I returned, she was on a respirator. She had had minor, additional bleeding; but it was believed that her throat may have been scratched by the tube. Because she had fought the respirator, she had to be sedated. Since she did bite the tube quite hard, a mouthpiece had been inserted to prevent the possibility of her biting a hole through it. For now, this was her lifeline; but she never spoke again.

Next day she stabilized; and on the 16th, the respirator was shut down for fifteen minutes without her relapse. Next, the type of respirator was changed to one that compensated only for breathing which she could not do independently. Machine assistance continued until she was removed from it by the evening of July 18. The physicians were exultant; it was the first time such a case had been successfully disconnected from a respirator.

Lisa's night was restless, one with much mumbling and apparent abdominal discomfort; but she said nothing clearly enough to be understood and shook her head, *No*, to all inquiries. Pain medications quieted her agitations. Next morning she held fairly steady. She seemed exhausted because breathing had been such hard work.

Late afternoon of July 20, her temperature shot up. Unrecognized by us at the time, this signaled the onset of a total collapse. A sharp change in mental alertness denoted the possibility of central nervous system involvement. If the scheduled spinal tap revealed a problem, it would be treatable; it would not imply brain damage or a permanent disorder. The tap was completely clear; the reduction in Lisa's acuteness most likely was due to her high fever.

Far from home, with no anticipation of seeing anyone we knew, unexpected visitors sometimes surprised us during our stay at Johns Hopkins—neighbors and friends, on vacation or in the area on business, even Dr. J—, one of Lisa's physicians from St. Jude. How we needed their unannounced visits, especially when hometown friends arrived July 20. Their presence for the next 48 hours was a miracle of ministry to us.

We waited until late that evening to dine with them, after assurances from the hospital staff that Lisa was resting comfortably. When we returned, I again stayed the night, dozing in a chair in the hall or sitting beside her bed. The situation remained unchanged next morning, but Lisa certainly had come through another crisis of some sort. Minor encouragement, again.

On this particular day, the entire floor of the hospital moved up one level to permit needed repair work. I took Lisa's belongings to her new room and fixed her bulletin board. Her physician was to accompany her transfer.

Before I left the hospital to get some rest, I told Lisa that the doctor had commented "how much improved" she was this morning; and I explained that soon she would be moving upstairs. "Don't try to talk," I said. "If you understand, just nod your head. I know you are very sick," I went on, "but things *are* better today. Just hang on." Then I repeated the words that I often used when I left her. "Remember, keep your finger on the boat."

She turned toward me and opened her eyes. She had always hung on to that encouraging thought given to her years earlier by my friend Juliann in Memphis: Even if the boat capsizes, you will not drown as long as you still can touch it. Lisa nodded, *Yes.*

I went to my room, showered, then tried to sleep. I could not relax. Gene sat with Lisa in her new room until noon when we went to lunch with our friends.

When we returned about 2:00 p. m., Lisa's room was overflowing with medical personnel. The nursing supervisor asked us to sit down; the problem would be explained shortly. It was obvious that we were not needed in the room; and there was no space anyway, so we sat in the hall.

Lisa had suffered total collapse: heart stoppage, blood pressure drop, cessation of breathing. They had revived her, but she was unconscious and back on the respirator.

Technically, she may have been alive; but Lisa was dead. A doctor emerged from her room, put his hand on Gene's shoulder and said, "Prayer, just prayer."

We sat, waited, wept. We heard the respirator stop. The door opened and Lisa's physician came out. "I am sorry. Lisa is dead."

A part of us died with her. I felt totally exhausted, more zombie than person. Lisa's ordeal was over. I felt as if ours was just beginning.

"Goodbye," she said.
"I love you so much.
We don't tell each other
Often enough."
Her message to the world,
To her family and friends.

To have lived so few years,
Loved so deeply,
Suffered so much,
And still leave
A message of Love,
This, truly, is living
For and with God.

V. Y. P.

ABOUT THE CO-AUTHOR

An Iowan from birth, Virginia Y. Pugh majored in child development at Iowa State University and was graduated with a degree in home economics. Married while still in college, she became a full-time homemaker and mother of three girls and two boys. When all were in school, and for the next twenty-two years, she also was a preschool teacher and director. Active in study groups, PEO and her church, she enjoys camping, reading, cooking, bridge, and the company of eight grandchildren.

After the death of Lisa, their fourth child, Virginia and her husband, Gene, were instrumental in organizing the first support group, in their community, for families of children with serious illness or for those who had suffered the death of a child. She has received an award for volunteer service to support St. Jude Children's Research Hospital and presents programs, particularly to high school and service organizations, on grief and the death of a child.

Acknowledgements

Bangs, John Kendrick, *The Foothills of Parnassus,* New York: Macmillan Publishing Company, 1914.

Guest, Edgar A., *Collected Verse of Edgar A. Guest,* New York: Contemporary Books, 1934. Used by permission of the publisher.

Hughes, Langston, *Random House Book of Poetry for Children,* New York: Random House, 1983. Used by permission of the publisher and Alfred A. Knopf, Inc.

Scollard, Clinton, *The Golden Book of Religious Verse,* Compiled by Thomas Curtis Clark, New York: Garden City Publishing Co., Inc., 1931. Used by permission of his literary heir, Nellie Rittenhouse Valley.

Wilcox, Ella Wheeler, *Poems That Touch the Heart,* Compiled by A. L. Alexander, New York: Doubleday & Co. and Checkerboard Press, 1956. Used by permission of the publisher.

Also, Camp Fire Inc., Kansas City, MO

ORDER KEEP YOUR FINGER ON THE BOAT
by Lisa Pugh and Virginia Y. Pugh

FROM −aP
−ana Publishing
Post Office Box 625
Kalamazoo, MI 49005

$8.95 Retail plus $1.55 Postage and
Handling. Michigan Addresses Add
$.36 Sales Tax

ALSO ORDER AFTER STEPHEN: From Hurting to Healed
by Norma R. Lantz
A mother's journal written after the
death of her young adult son

AVAILABLE FROM −aP
−ana Publishing
Post Office Box 625
Kalamazoo, MI 49005

$9.95 Retail, plus $1.55 Postage and
Handling. Michigan Addresses Add
$.40 Sales Tax